Enjoy the
adventure!
always,
Jerry

D1519335

As You Lie There... Sleeping

—— Terry I. Miles ——

iUniverse, Inc.
New York Bloomington

As You Lie There... Sleeping

iUniverse books may be ordered through booksellers or by contacting:

iUniverse
1663 Liberty Drive
Bloomington, IN 47403
www.iuniverse.com
1-800-Authors (1-800-288-4677)

Because of the dynamic nature of the Internet, any Web addresses or links contained in this book may have changed since publication and may no longer be valid. The views expressed in this work are solely those of the author and do not necessarily reflect the views of the publisher, and the publisher hereby disclaims any responsibility for them.

ISBN: 978-1-4401-6887-1 (pbk)
ISBN: 978-1-4401-6888-8 (ebook)

Printed in the United States of America

iUniverse rev. date:: 09/23/09

List of Characters

Ms Bea Winslow, private investigator.

Mrs. Julia Carter Buchanan McKenna, fondly called Aunt Jewels.

Sheriff Jim Travis, Sheriff of Lafouchfeye County and Bea's fiancé.

Sheriff Cecil Travis, deceased father of Jim Travis.

Rufus Cuevas, railroad yard inspector.

Old McDermott, railroad yard inspector.

Captain Eric VonBoatner, Captain of the Coral Princess and Aunt Jewels' boyfriend.

Percy (Teaspoon) Dinwiddle, owner of the Dinwiddle's Quik Stop

Horatio Clyde Lipton, manager of the Dinwiddle's Quik Stop.

Taylor L. Lipton, lawyer and youngest son of Clyde Lipton.

Judge Joseph P. Wallace and his wife Lindsey murdered in August, 1987.

District Attorney Wendell M. Holmes Jr., of Warren County and his wife Emma.

Retired Judge Roscoe Blackledge, old friend of Aunt Jewels.

Retired Judge Wendell M. Holmes Sr., of Lafouchfeye County.

Retired Judge Randall Penton and his wife Eloise of Lafouchfeye County.

Malcolm Blackledge, lawyer and son of Roscoe Blackledge

Huett R. Cuevas, lawyer.

Judge Ruben Glasglow of Jackson.

Mary Beth, Judge Glasglow's secretary.

Ralph, Judge Glasglow's confidant.

Judge Robert Kipper and his wife Cherie.

Stuart, Retired Judge Holmes' butler.

Molly, Retired Judge Holmes' housekeeper.

Matilda Pettigrew, business woman and 'confidant' of the Judge's.

Cahill Pettigrew, relative of Matilda.

FBI Special Agent Jack Thomas.

Dr. Nathan Tate, Forensic Pathologist of New Orleans, La.

Alex Dedeaux, Assistant to Dr. Tate.

Mrs. Lucy Dinwiddle Dupree, Bank employee.

Deputy Tatum, Deputy Paulie and Auxiliary Deputy Necaise.

Mr. Thaddeus Underwood of Syracuse, New York.

Contents

Acknowledgement

What I find fascinating about writing a book, novel or story, is the contact with a variety of diverse people and personalities. Everyone is very helpful with the research and ideas. Of course, in the acknowledgements their name is mentioned and they love that!

Take for example my friend Lucy. She is a friend and a dedicated writer of southern historical romance and mystery. We are always introduced as 'the mystery twins'. She writes the more sensual, juicy romance, whereas I dabble in the innuendo. That being said, we were relaxing over a hot cup of java at Barnes & Noble when a couple approached. They were friends of Lucy's. The gentleman was introduced to me as United States District Judge Louis Guirola Jr. After Lucy told him about my Cozy Little Murder Mysteries, he had a suggestion. He 'requested' that my next story, not only have a judge get killed, but have the killer be a judge.

The germ of an idea was planted! Of course, I demurely smiled and replied, "you have to have more than one or two judges in the story."

He nodded his head in agreement. After he and his wife walked away, Lucy said, "Terry, are you going to tell the readers who the killer is right off the bat?"

I smiled again. "No, no way. I just have to invent a story with several judges...retired, active and disbarred!"

Let me thank Richard and Dee Cichon for their faithful work, my friend Evelyn who has enjoyed my readings of tidbits of the story over coffee and croissants at Burger King, my three adult children, Rusty, Holly and Susan and my faithful readers in Arkansas, North Carolina, Texas, Mississippi, Illinois, Ohio, Indiana and yes, even Africa!

Oops! I almost forgot one more very important person! Ms Annette Copeland, itech guru!

Without her expertise, I would be lost!

So sit back and enjoy the mystery, suspense and humor of Aunt Jewels, her niece Bea Winslow, the private investigator and Bea's fiancé, Sheriff of Lafouchfeye County, Jim Travis, and the rest of Terry's imagination of characters.

Synopsis

Lafouchfeye County, Mississippi, and the entire Mississippi Gulf Coast were still reeling from the double murder in August of 1987 of a distinguished Judge and his wife, when a week before Christmas of the same year, the newlywed couple of recently elected District Attorney Wendell Matthew Holmes, Jr. of Warren County, Mississippi, and his wife Emma, are discovered dead in a refrigerator car in the Lafouchfeye County railroad yard by Rufus Cuevas, a railroad inspector.

Percy (Teaspoon) Dinwiddle was found guilty of the Holmes' murders and sentenced to thirty years in prison. He protested his innocence. At the time, Sheriff Cecil Travis wondered, *were the two separate homicides connected?* The first case went unsolved, Sheriff Travis died of a heart attack and after the first of the year, his son, Jim Travis was elected Sheriff on January 6, 1988.

Twenty years later a young lawyer named Taylor L. Lipton was researching both sets of homicides and new evidence through DNA was introduced concerning Percy Dinwiddle. Percy was set free on February 1 of 2009.

On February 17th, 2009, Private Investigator Bea Winslow and her Aunt Julia McKenna, whom she fondly calls Aunt Jewels, are driving home from Jackson, Mississippi after attending a Recognition Banquet for Lawyers and Judges.

Just inside of the Lafouchfeye County line, Bea filled up her gas tank and Aunt Jewels bought a cool drink at Dinwiddle's Quick Stop. Their continued drive was delayed by a stopped train. After several minutes, Aunt Jewels observed an elderly man jumping from one of the railroad cars. As Bea shined her spot light, she spied a bloody hand dangling out of the boxcar door.

Immediately Bea called her fiancée Jim Travis, the Sheriff of Lafouchfeye County. Was this a copycat of the December 1987 homicide or a connection of the unsolved murders four months earlier?

Greed, revenge, and deception erupt like a volcano, throwing Jim, Bea and Aunt Jewels into a whirlwind of chaos.

Prologue

December 22, 1987

The refrigerator car was barely visible through the wafting fog as it lingered over the track at the west end in the Lafouchfeye County, Mississippi railroad yard. Except for the occasional staccato bark of a stray dog, the silence was deadly. Their meeting with him was tainted.

Funny, he didn't feel any remorse. After killing them, he repacked his automatic pistol into its case and slowly opened the heavy door with his gloved hand. It had to be done. They knew too much. After all, they were connected and the connection had to be severed.

He glanced in both directions and then hopped down, twisting his right ankle while landing in the loose gravel. He cursed.

The bobbing beam of a flashlight protruding through the fog brought him upright. Quickly he hobbled to his vehicle. He'd parked on the other side of the fence in the grassy knoll.

His entire leg now throbbed while sitting inside his car. His eyes strained to watch Rufus Cuevas, the railroad inspector, making his rounds. The killer's adrenalin was pumping and he smiled through his pain, waiting for their bodies to be discovered.

As Rufus approached the refrigerator car, he noticed two things. The large door was open and the freezing unit wasn't running.   He gripped the middle rung of the slim metal bars that formed a vertical line on the opposite side and pulled himself up. Obviously the unit had been off for awhile, for inside it was warm and moist.

He shined his flashlight toward the wall and flicked the switch. Instantly it kicked on. *I wonder,* he thought, *what was wrong?*

Turning completely around, his flashlight caught sight of the two dead bodies lying facing each other. Behind them, cartons of melted ice cream, popsicles and ice cream sandwiches oozed out of broken packages. His gut clenched. Immediately he recognized the couple as the newly elected District Attorney Wendell Matthew Holmes, Jr. and his beautiful wife, Emma, of Warren County. Rufus had been friends with the Holmes family for years. Wendell Holmes, Sr. was a retired Lafouchfeye County Federal Judge.

Their bodies had been arranged. Rufus could tell they had been dragged to their final position. Their hands were tied behind their backs. As Rufus shined his light back and forth over the couple, his eyes caught sight of a perfect footprint in the pool of blood coming from the young lady's head.

Rufus started backing up and stumbled over a three legged milking stool. Before he regained his balance, his flashlight lit up the ceiling of the car and then shined on the floor. He saw the butt of a cigar immersed in melted chocolate at the dead man's feet and a strawberry stained crumpled up piece of paper. He snatched it up and stuffed it in his pocket. Quickly he jumped down to the ground and hurried to his yard shack to call Sheriff Cecil Travis.

As the killer watched Rufus run back, he popped a pain pill in his mouth and washed it down with whiskey. Slowly he backed up his BMW. On the final curve into town, he passed the Sheriff and his deputy.

Present Time

CHAPTER ONE

Aunt Jewels' House

"Aunt Jewels," asked Bea, "have you got the paper?"

"What, dear?"

"The paper, where is it?"

"I don't know."

"You had it last."

Peering over her glasses, Aunt Jewels' eyes darted around the living room. She spied a torn section of it tucked behind the edge of the sofa. "Dear, I think Ramses has it."

"You, I, and that dog are going to go two hands around."

"Now don't get yourself in a dither over a newspaper."

"It's not just the newspaper. Yesterday, it was one of my good house slippers. Last week he was chewing on my potting gloves."

Aunt Jewels grinned. "Dear, he's just a puppy."

"No, he's six years old. It's time he grew up."

Aunt Jewels reached down and picked up the snowy white poodle. "Remember, he was a Christmas gift from our friends."

Rolling her eyes, Bea picked up the different sections of The Lafouchfeye Ledger. "How could I forget?"

"What's in there that you want to see?"

"Maude's write ups about the banquet and the bodies of that couple found in the railroad car."

"Oh."

"How come, you're not interested?"

"I have other things on my mind."

"Really? And what might that be?"

"A certain gentleman might be calling me."

"I take it you're not talking about Eric?"

"That's correct."

"So, it must be someone you just met, like Mr. Jack Thomas, the FBI Agent."

Aunt Jewels' eyes sparkled. "Uh...huh. But, if you need my assistance..."

Bea smiled. "I'll certainly let you know. Here's the article about the banquet in Jackson."

Local Lawyers and Judges Recognized at Banquet in Jackson, Mississippi

Retired Federal Judges, Randall Scott Penton, Roscoe Blackledge and Wendell Matthew Holmes, Sr. were recognized at the recent banquet in the Marriott Hotel Ballroom for their distinguished service. The lawyers involved in what became known as The Katrina Project were Malcolm Blackledge, Taylor Upton and Huett Raleigh Cuevas. These three lawyers did exceptional service to their profession and their state.

Maude Benson The Lafouchfeye Ledger

"I was surprised to see Roscoe there."

Bea stopped peeling potatos. "Me too. I didn't know he had a son."

"Roscoe's been gone for twenty some years, Bea. He left right after Jimmy and me were married."

"Are you implying Roscoe was sweet on you? You always said he was sweet on momma."

"Yes dear, he was. Both of us. But when your mom and dad married, well he figured he had to get away. So he went to China."

Bea turned, pointing the potato peeler towards her Aunt. "But he came back when you were on trial for the murder of my father."

"That's right."

"So, who is Malcolm's mother?"

"Was, dear, was. Roscoe told me at the banquet, he'd married a missionary living in China. After the three of them boarded the ferry to go to the mainland, a storm came up and capsized the boat. Roscoe saved Malcolm, but his wife, Paulette, drowned. Malcolm was three."

"He never remarried?"

"Not that I know of."

"Roscoe is still a handsome gentleman."

Her aunt snickered a little. "Did you find the article about the two bodies in the stopped railroad car?"

"Yes, here it is."

"Did Maude mention us?"

"Yes."

"Has Jim identified them yet?"

"No, the acid did its job."

Aunt Jewels grimaced. "I hope they were dead."

"Me, too. But a killer doesn't care about the pain he inflicts."

"Was there any identification?"

"No, not even a credit card, but Jim did mention a wadded-up scrap of paper."

Bodies Found in Railroad Car While Train is Stopped in Lafouchfeye County.

On February 17, while returning from a banquet in Jackson, Mississippi, Ms Bea Winslow, Private Investigator, and her Aunt, Julia McKenna, discovered the remains of a young couple, shot in the head. Mrs. McKenna saw an elderly man jump from the boxcar and Ms Winslow notified Sheriff Jim Travis of Lafouchfeye County. No further details are known at this time.

Maude Benson The Lafouchfeye Ledger

CHAPTER TWO

Dinwiddle's Quik Stop The Next Morning

"Teaspoon, is that you rummagin' around in the stock room?" Clyde yelled. My name is Horatio Clyde Lipton and it was my son, Taylor L. Lipton that proved Teaspoon didn't kill that Attorney fella and his wife over twenty years ago.

Now Teaspoon was Percy's nickname he'd acquired as a child. Every time his momma would carry him to his Uncle, Judge Chester Dinwiddle's court, when Chester pounded his gavel, Percy would bang his teaspoon on the polished wooden railing. His momma was hopin' he'd follow in his Uncle's footsteps and he did, but he got into trouble later on.

His Christian name was Percy Chester Dinwiddle, born and bred in Lafouchfeye County, Mississippi. His grand pappy and pappy had owned and operated this little Quik Stop grocery store for over a hundred years. Why I can recall Teapsoon tellin' us kids tales about the Indians trading beaver pelts for bacon and beans. However, some of the Dinwiddle's went to college, became lawyers, judges and even opened a funeral parlor in the next county.

Although Teaspoon was a tad older, we had been friends since grade school, and I was there everyday of his trial. Later on my youngest son, Taylor L., who became a lawyer, visited him at Angola Prison in

Louisiana each weekend. I've been takin' care of Dinwiddle's Quik Stop for nye over twenty years. I was happy that Taylor was following in my footsteps. In two years he was planning on running for Circuit Court Judge.

"Were you yellin' for me awhile ago, Clyde?"

"Yeah, Teaspoon. What'cha doin' back there?"

"Lookin' for somethin'."

"Have you seen the paper?"

"Yep."

"What'cha think?"

"About what?"

"Finding that couple dead in one of the boxcars."

Teaspoon grinned. "It don't affect me."

"It said Mrs. McKenna saw an elderly man jump out of the railroad
car."

Teaspoon limped over to Clyde. "It wasn't me."

"Yeah, yeah, Teaspoon. But you know how some people are."

"Look, I served twenty years. Your youngin' got me out. He proved it in court."

Just then, Sheriff Jim Travis drove up in his dilapidated Jeep.

"Howdy, Sheriff," said Clyde. "What brings you up to these parts?"

The Sheriff looked directly at Teaspoon. "I need to ask you some questions."

"About what?"

"Where were you last night between ten and eleven p.m.?"

"I was nowhere near that railroad track, I can tell you that."

"Teaspoon, I'm trying to help you."

"By puttin' me in that there vicinity?"

"Just tell him where you were, Teaspoon," pleaded Clyde. "He was at my house, Sheriff. We were watchin' wrestlin' on T.V."

Jim looked down at Teaspoon's shoes. "You mind if I check them?"

"Yeah, I do mind, because it was my shoe print in that icebox car that help send me up the first time! I was stupid for getting' drunk and crawlin' in there in the first place.   I tell ya, I wasn't anywhere around the tracks last night."

The Sheriff ambled over by the end of the glass counter. "Teaspoon, I talked to Elsie, the bar maid. She told me you were at the Town Tavern till about nine o'clock. Old McDermott, the railroad inspector saw you in the railroad yard around ten."

"Okay. I got drunk and I took the short cut through the railroad yard."

"Teaspoon, let him have your shoes," said Clyde.

"Aw here. Take 'em."

"Thanks, Teaspoon. I'll check them out with the plaster cast I have back at my office," the Sheriff replied.

"Need anything else, Sheriff?" Clyde asked.

"Clyde, myself and Dr. Nathan Tate, the Forensic Pathologist out of New Orleans, Louisiana, have identified the young man and woman who were murdered and found in that boxcar."

Teaspoon sighed deeply.

"Who were they?" Clyde asked.

"Clyde, that's the other reason I drove out. I hate to tell you this. It was Taylor, your youngest son and his wife, Laurie. I'll tell Dr. Tate you'll be getting in touch with him for the final arrangements."

Clyde and Teaspoon stood there, stunned.

After Sheriff Travis drove off, Teaspoon looked helplessly down at the holes in his socks and then at Clyde. "Clyde? Why did you lie?"

CHAPTER THREE

The Office of Sheriff Jim Travis

Sheriff Jim Travis panted heavily into his land phone. "I caught you home, Bea. Good."

"What have you been doing?"

"Running. Your Aunt drove into town and dropped by to see me. When Ramses, her little dog, saw Spooky, my black cat, you can imagine what happened."

Bea laughed. "So, who did you catch? Aunt Jewels, the dog or your cat?"

"Actually the dog. Aunt Jewels wanted me to tell you she'd be home after she handled a couple of errands."

"Jim, what do you need?"

"I asked Judge Holmes if we could pay him a visit, but first I'd like you to drop by my office."

"Why do you want 'us' to see him, Jim?"

I dug out my Father's old files, you know, about Judge Holmes' son's death. This homicide is similar."

"Okay, I'll leave Aunt Jewels a note, here at the house and be on my way."

"See you soon. Bye."

* *

When Bea entered his office, Jim's face lit up like a Christmas tree. "Come here," he urged.

Willingly, Bea stepped forward and nestled between his outstretched arms. "Hummmm, that feels good."

"I needed this hug," said Jim.

Still holding him close, Bea whispered in his ear, "Why do you want us to see old man Holmes? He seemed like a stuffed shirt at the banquet in Jackson."

Jim smirked and pulled back a little. "He can afford to be a stuffed shirt, honey. That's why his house is not a home. It's a chateau. Look at my dad's file on his son's death."

Bea unwrapped her arms from Jim and sat down at his desk. Every once in awhile she'd glance up and look at him as she read the sheath of paperwork. "What's this?"

"What's what?"

Bea held up a small crumbled-up piece of yellowed paper. "Looks like the verse to a song or poem."

"My dad refers to it in his notes. It seems Rufus found it in the refrigerator car by the dead man's feet. He stuck it in his pocket and then later on gave it to my dad."

"Hummm," said Bea. "Maybe there's a connection." Gently Bea pressed on the small wrinkled note and read it to herself. *'If it be winter's cold retreat, my frozen bier will moan, and as you lie there sleeping, My love will soon be home.'* "Jim?"

"Yes?"

"Do you have one of those little plastic sandwich bags?"

"I think so, why?"

"Because I want to save this from excessive handling. After all, it is over twenty years old."

"Here you are."

"Thanks." Carefully, she slipped the paper inside, turned over the plastic sheath and began smoothing the clasp together. Suddenly she stopped. "Jim, come here."

"What is it?"

Bea slowly opened the sealed bag and retrieved the wrinkled piece of torn paper. "Jim, hand me your magnifying glass."

"What do you see?"

"I missed it before because it's more prominent on the back side. Looking at the enlargement, I can vaguely make out three numbers and five letters."

"Yes, yes, I see them. It looks like a five, seven and eight."

Bea undid a paper clip and pointed it toward each number. "That could be an eight, one and three. The letters are backward." She held it up towards the light. "It looks like H C P P C. Or that first C, could be a O."

"What'ya think it is?" asked Jim.

Bea slipped it inside the bag once more. "It could be a safety deposit box number and where it's located." After several minutes, Bea closed the yellowed manila folder. "I'm thinking of something else. Do you think Wendell Holmes had something to do with his son's death?"

"Yes, it's a possibility. Just reading my father's notes makes me wonder."

"Wonder about what?"

"Dad's death."

"Your father's? You don't think Judge Holmes..."

"Bea, my pop didn't have heart problems. He was healthy as a horse. And... the Judge could be involved with the homicides we found the other evening. Look, I had to inform Clyde Lipton, it was his son and daughter-in- law I found dead in that boxcar, and I also picked up Dinwiddle's shoes from him. Bea, the plaster cast I made at the crime scene wasn't a match."

"How did you and Dr. Tate find out who they were?"

"Obviously the killer didn't notice or look at Taylor Lipton's cuff links or check his wife's purse. Inside we found a small testament inscribed to Laurie Lipton by her father in law. She had received it when they were married. It was the something 'new' part. Plus the killer disfigured them."

"Jim?"

"Yeah?"

"Let me see the folder you have on Taylor and Laurie Lipton. Didn't you say you found a wadded-up piece of paper?"

"Here's the file. It's in a plastic sheath, toward the back."

"Here it is." She carefully removed it and began reading out loud. *"If it be springtime when I pass, The daffodils will mourn, And as you lie there sleeping, My soul will be forlorn.* Jim, I've heard these words, but I can't recall where. Let me look at the little white testament. Jim..."

"What?"

"Would you look at this?"

Bea held up the small book. "Don't you think it's odd that only one page is folded down and it's page 578."

"Bea, do you think there's a connection?"

"More than ever now." As she picked up the two manila folders, an old newspaper clipping slipped out. "What's this?"

Jim read the bold print: **Estate Jewels Missing.** "It must have fallen out of dad's documents. Look at the date."

August 31, 1987

During the estate sale of Mary Necaise Dedeaux, sister of Lucy Shuttlesworth Cuevas, it appears that several priceless jewels were misplaced. The two items in question are a brooch and a gold bracelet. For further details, contact Sheriff Cecil Travis, Lafouchfeye County.

"Jim, why did he keep this with the Wallace murder documents?"

"Beats me."

"Obviously, it has something to do with it."

"Well, I think Judge Holmes is involved. Instead of a Judge getting killed, I'm thinking a Judge did the killing."

"But we don't know why."

"Bea, are you ready to get on this merry-go-round and go for a spin?"

After giving him a big bear hug and a peck, Bea added, "lead the way!"

CHAPTER FOUR

The Chateau of Wendell Matthew Holmes

As Jim meandered his Jeep around the circled driveway, Bea reached across and nudged his shoulder. "This is some layout. Have you ever been inside?"

"Nope," he replied.

"I think we're both in for a treat," she winked.

After parking in the designated spot, they ambled up the cobblestone steps. Bea reached up to the attached large brass ship's bell and rang it.

Slowly opening the massive metal door, the butler replied coldly, "Good morning. Please follow me. I will inform Judge Holmes you have arrived and he will join you on the back veranda in a moment."

Bea took a quick survey of the foyer. "Judge Holmes has a lovely home."

The butler stopped sharply and turned. "Chateau, madam. He prefers the word, chateau."

"I stand corrected. Chateau it is."

"Would you care for a cup of tea or coffee?"

"I would prefer coffee," said Jim.

"Me too," Bea added.

"Please, make yourselves comfortable."

Jim watched the butler leave and then looked across the lush green lawn that stretched out before him. "Man, this is some layout. You could really knock a golf ball around on that manicured acre of ground."

Bea joined him on the extended marble balcony. "I'd say the Judge has had a very, very comfortable life, wouldn't you?"

"Ah, there you are. Good morning, Sheriff Travis and it is Ms Winslow, isn't it?" greeted Judge Holmes.

"Thank you very much for inviting us to your home, I mean chateau, sir," replied Jim. "My fiancée, Bea and I appreciate you taking the time out of your busy schedule to see us."

"You forget Sheriff, I'm retired. I make my own time. Congratulations, I didn't know you were engaged."

"Thank you," said Bea. "And you have a gorgeous place to spend your time."

"I have to credit my late wife and daughter-in-law for the designing of the outside garden area and Ms Matilda Pettigrew of Jackson for the interior of the chateau. Now, how can I be of assistance?"

"Of course Judge, you read in the paper about Bea and her Aunt discovering the unfortunate homicide the other evening."

"The boxcar incident. Yes, tragic. Just tragic. Do you have any leads?"

"That's why I'm here, Judge Holmes. I'm sorry to bring up unpleasant memories, but this present case has some similarities to the homicides of your son and daughter-in-law over twenty years ago."

"How so?"

"For starters, in a railroad car. The first one was a refrigerator car and of course this one was a boxcar. Both couples were young. Your son was a newly elected District Attorney. The present case involved a young lawyer, who recently had Percy Dinwiddle freed with new evidence of DNA."

"And do you believe the two are connected?"

Even though the Judge was looking at the Sheriff, Bea replied, "We do."

Judge Holmes immediately focused his attention on her. "And why is that, Ms Winslow?"

"I read Jim's father's file on your son's murder. He was involved in an undercover sting of the illegal gambling, prostitution and racketeering

12

along the Mississippi Gulf Coast with a number of other elected officials, including several mayors, plus judges, lawyers and councilmen."

Judge Holmes stroked his chin. "I agree with you Ms Winslow. Since my son was the newly elected District Attorney of Warren County, he was 'involved' as you so eloquently put it. I do believe the authorities rounded them up, at least I remember reading about it in the Lafouchfeye Ledger or something to that effect. They even wrote a book about it."

"You are correct; Judge Holmes and some are still in prison. That is precisely the reason, and we believe anyway, that Clyde Lipton's son, Taylor, and his wife were killed. Because he proved Percy Dinwiddle was innocent and someone else committed those murders. That person is still free."

Leaning forward, the Judge asked, "Which homicide are you referring to?"

Bea didn't blink. "All of them."

"Even the double murder of Judge Wallace and his wife?"

"Yes sir. The way I see it, the police and authorities hit a dead end with the Wallace killings, but your son obviously discovered some crucial evidence and unfortunately, he and his wife had to be eliminated. Percy Dinwiddle was framed for their murder, so the original killer was... and is still free. When attorney Taylor Lipton started investigating Percy's conviction, obviously he came across evidence concerning the 1987 murders and both he and his wife had to be killed."

"Sheriff Travis, your fiancée has a vivid imagination. She should be a teacher or storyteller," said Holmes, pointing his cigar. "She reminds me of your father, Cecil. Now there was a blood hound if I ever saw one. He would pick up a scent and run with it. There was one time when he interrupted my court and insisted on talking to me in my chambers."

Jim's face turned ashen grey. "Yes sir, I recall that day and evening. After seeing you, he returned to his office. Thirty minutes later, he had a heart attack and died."

Judge Holmes took a sip of his coffee. "Yes Jim, I couldn't believe he was gone. Just that fast. Tragic, so very tragic."

"We won't take any more of your time, Judge. We just wanted you to know we were going over all the events from back then.   If you can remember any pertinent information, just let me or Bea know. We'd appreciate that."

"Stuart?" Judge Holmes called.

A short plump woman appeared, holding a large feather duster. "Yes sir."

In an agitated tone, Judge Holmes asked, "Where's Stuart, Molly?"

"Sir, Mr. Stuart is tending to a disturbance on the side terrace."

"Disturbance?"

"Yes sir. I believe some teenagers ran into your rose bushes on their bicycles."

"I see. Molly will show you to the door. Thank you again for coming, Sheriff and Ms Winslow. I hope to see you soon under more pleasant circumstances."

"Please follow me," said Molly. "You're Mrs. McKenna's niece, aren't you?"

"Yes I am."

"Please say hello for me. The name is Molly McGuire. I belong to the Garden Club also. I haven't made the last several meetings. I've been busy, you know. Tell her I have some fresh vegetables. I'd be happy to bring them by."

"I'll certainly tell her. Molly, that's a lovely framed piece of poetry. Is it a family heirloom of Judge Holmes'?" Bea inquired.

Molly stifled a giggle. "Mercy no, ma'am. I believe Ms Pettigrew picked it up at an auction in Jackson."

"Well, it's very interesting."

As Molly ushered the two of them out the front door, Judge Holmes bellowed loudly, "Molly, come here!"

CHAPTER FIVE

Roscoe Blackledge Visits Aunt Jewels

As Bea approached the turnoff, she spotted a dark blue sedan parked in the shade of the front oak tree of Aunt Jewels' house. Driving slowly by, she noticed it was a Mississippi tag from Warren County. That was the Vicksburg area. *Who could that be,* she thought. "Yoo hoo, I'm home Aunt Jewels."

"In the living room, dear. We have a guest."

Smiling, Bea entered and saw a tall, distinguished gentleman standing, with soft white hair and black framed spectacles. "Hello."

"Dear, you remember Judge Roscoe Blackledge? From the banquet, in Jackson?"

"Why of course. So nice of you to visit. I hope Aunt Jewels has remembered her entertaining manners."

He smiled and sat back down beside her. "She still looks as lovely and sweet as ever."

"Hush Roscoe. You'll make me blush."

"Of course, you'll stay for dinner."

"Only if Julia makes her infamous spaghetti and meatballs with garlic butter bread."

"That can be arranged. I happen to know my fiancé loves that dish also."

"Sheriff Travis, correct?" said Roscoe.

"That's right."

"Julia was telling me of your discovery the other evening."

"About?"

"The stopped train." He grabbed Julia's hand. "She has the eyes of an eagle, you know. Spotting that man jumping out of the boxcar."

"Roscoe, even though he was elderly, he was spry. That's quite a leap, you know."

He let out a boisterous laugh. "Julia, I haven't jumped out of very many railroad cars."

"But Bea helped too. She shined her spot light and saw him."

"Aunt Jewels, if we want to eat before midnight, we had better begin cooking."

"You are so right, dear. Excuse us Roscoe, or you can join us in the kitchen."

"I think I will. I didn't get the chance to do much conversing at the banquet."

"That's right, Roscoe," said Aunt Jewels. "Those three men were certainly bending your ear. Who were they?"

"Julia, I was surrounded by Judges, lawyers and media all night long."

"Well now, I do know one of them. Judge Wendell Matthew Holmes Sr."

"He still lives in this county, doesn't he?"

"Yes, he does, Judge Blackledge," Bea answered.

"Please Bea, call me Roscoe."

She turned around and smiled. "I can remember calling you Uncle Roscoe."

He leaned back in the ladder back chair. "Please, don't remind me of my age. Young lady, when are we going to have a wedding?"

"Now you're sounding like my aunt."

Aunt Jewels winked. "That's what usually happens when you get engaged. Later on you get married."

Bea glanced at her and frowned. "Watch your spaghetti sauce."

"See how she treats me, Roscoe?"

"Listen Julia, after supper, how about going for a drive by Lake Bayou?"

"I'd like that. Well, look who just drove up! Jim Travis."

"Hello there folks. I'm glad you're here Judge Blackledge."

"What's up Jim?" Bea asked.

"Well, Clyde returned earlier with the bodies of his son and daughter-in-law. Dinwiddle's Funeral Services of Moriah County is conducting the closed casket services at ten a.m. tomorrow morning at The Lafouchfeye All Saints Chapel, just off of Highway 13. I just dropped by to let Aunt Jewels and Bea know. That's why I'm glad you're here, Judge. Saves me a phone call. If you need a place to spend the night, you can do it at my place."

"That's mighty kind of you Jim. I'll take you up on your offer. Julia, we'll have to postpone our drive. I'd better get these old bones to bed. See you tomorrow at the funeral."

Bea snuggled up next to Jim. "You have to leave so soon?"

He gave her a tight squeeze. "How about sittin' a spell in the back porch swing?"

"That sounds wonderful."

"Roscoe," cooed Julia, "let's have a nice hot cup of tea and pretend we're parked at Lake Bayou?"

A big grin appeared on Roscoe's face. "Jim, let me know when you're ready to leave."

"Will do."

CHAPTER SIX

Judge Randall Penton Visits Judge Holmes

"Judge Holmes?"

"Yes, Stuart?"

"Judge Penton is here to see you."

"Show him to the library. I'll be there shortly." Wendell returned to the back courtyard, walked up behind her and placed his huge hands on both her shoulders. "There's nothing for you to worry about. I'll take care of everything. I always have, haven't I?"

As she turned within his arms, he felt her sensual vibrations pass through his body. "Wendell, darling...," she whispered, while brushing his lips. "I'll see you later."

He watched her leave through the garden gate. Carefully he removed any trace of lipstick and stuck the hanky back in his jacket. "Stuart?" he called. "Could you bring me a brandy?" He mentally prepared his opening remarks while approaching the mahogany library door. "Randall, this is a pleasant surprise. What brings you to my neck of the woods?"

"As if you didn't know."

"Know? What is it that I'm supposed to know?"

"Lipton's dead and so is his wife."

"Oh, that unfortunate tragic event. Yes, I do know that."

"It's going to open up everything again."

"Randall, what are you talking about?"

"The murders. The investigation. Everything."

"Man, be specific."

"You know. Judge Joseph P. Wallace and his wife."

"Randall, would you like a drink? Sherry? Wine? Some brandy?"

"How can you be so calm?"

"Because there's nothing amiss."

"Wendell, Dinwiddle was supposed to stay in jail. Not to get out."

"I agree."

"That Sheriff is going to dig around."

Wendell smirked. "His father died in office and he can too. Randall, you won't have to soil your lily white hands again. By the way, Sheriff Travis and his fiancée visited me earlier."

"He was here? What did he want?"

Wendell shrugged his shoulders. "Just to introduce himself and ask for my help."

"Your help?"

"Yes, because of the similarity of the homicides."

"How does he want your help?"

"You forget it was my son and daughter-in-law that were murdered."

Randall bristled. "I haven't forgotten. Emma was my daughter."

Wendell took a small sip of brandy. "How's your wife, Eloise?"

Randall got up and ambled toward the large bay window overlooking the garden. "She's visiting her Aunt Lucy in Biloxi. I'm supposed to meet her for lunch at Mary Mahoney's."

"Please, give her my best."

Randall continued to gaze out of the window. "I will Wendell, I'll tell her you asked about her."

CHAPTER SEVEN

Attorney Malcolm Blackledge

Malcolm was the spitting image of his father, Roscoe when he was a younger man. His black curly hair and rugged good looks made him the most eligible bachelor in Jackson, but his pleasure for a mature woman was what set him apart.

As he sailed the small schooner thru the gulf waters, Malcolm recalled the first time his father took him sailing. He was twelve and it was the Li River in China, near Gulin, (Guay-lin). The wooden dingy weaved and rocked as it cut through the choppy green water. Malcolm had a hard time keeping the rudder trim, but Roscoe was right by his side offering encouragement.

Now gripping the lacquered schooner steering wheel, he couldn't help but remember the instant change in his father's demeanor when he found out about their mutual friends' death. Roscoe had been Taylor's mentor during law school.

He told Malcolm he was renting a car and driving to Lafouchfeye County to see an old friend. Also he asked Malcolm to please bring the boat down. He felt the sail back home to Jackson would be relaxing for him. Malcolm decided he would drop in and see Clyde, Taylor's father. As he pulled up his rental car in front of the Quik Stop, he noticed the tasteful black wreath hanging off to the side. Seeing Mr. Dinwiddle, Malcolm acknowledged his presence. "Hello there."

"Howdy do, Malcolm. What brings you down this way?"

"I'm meeting my father later at the Gulfport Yacht Club and I thought I'd stop by and pay my respects to Clyde."

Teaspoon shook his head. "Yeah, that was a tough one to take."

"Is he doing okay?"

"As best as can be expected, I guess."

"Sheriff Travis working the case?"

"Uh-huh."

"Any leads?"

"Not that I know of. He did come out here though and got my shoes."

"Why?"

"Well, I guess the fella that jumped out of the boxcar left his footprints. They weren't mine."

"That's what sent you up last time, right?"

"Uh huh."

Malcolm grinned. "I know Taylor was excited when he knew for sure you were getting out of Angola."

"We both were. I'm mighty grateful to Mr. Lipton."

"Look," said Malcolm, "I'd love to stay and chat with you, but I really must be heading toward the Coast. Tell Clyde I stopped by."

As Malcolm started for his car, his cell phone rang. "Hello? Yes, this is a pleasant surprise. No, he wasn't there. I don't think you have anything to worry about. I know, I know. Look, I'll mention it, okay? I'm on my way now. No, I didn't know. I'll attend, though. Bye."

CHAPTER EIGHT

Lafouchfeye All Saints Chapel Funeral for Mr. and Mrs. Taylor Lipton

The Sheriffs Jeep and Roscoe's car were already at the funeral home, when Bea and Aunt Jewels drove up. Aunt Jewels pulled down the visor and checked her makeup, and then she stepped out of the car.

"Aunt Jewels," called Bea. "Put my cell phone in your big bag."

"Okay, dear," she replied, but continued to hold it in her hand. "Hello, Roscoe. Did you sleep well?"

"Like a rock, Julia. Even Jim's snoring didn't bother me."

Bea smiled. "He does sound like a freight train sometimes."

Jim frowned. "You two go ahead and make fun, but I could tell some tales of a certain camping trip...."

"Okay, Jim," begged Bea. "I'm sorry."

"I thought you'd see it my way."

The funeral assistant greeted them with a broad smile. "Good morning, ladies and gentlemen. The services will be held in the Robert E. Lee Chapel."

"Thank you sir," replied Bea and Jim.

Roscoe and Aunt Jewels side-stepped Jim and Bea and walked into the fragrant parlor. Aunt Jewels looked at the lovely flower bouquets, mostly lilies, positioned around the two closed caskets. "Roscoe," whispered Aunt Jewels, "She was such a lovely young lady."

"Yes, she was. I was so sorry to hear of their untimely passing."

"Psst.., Aunt Jewels," said Bea, "Come sit down."

"Okay, okay. Mercy," she replied. No one noticed the cell phone had slipped from her fingers.

Quietly the Assistant Funeral Director approached the caskets. In a few minutes the services began.

Reverend Bowman read a few verses from the Bible as soft organ music softly played *'Come to The Garden'* in the background. Clyde Lipton spoke about his son's early years and his accomplishments. Brushing away the tears, he recalled meeting Laurie for the first time. She had been raised by her mother's sister and had recently lost her to a tragic accident. Clyde assured everyone that both Taylor and Laurie were together still in a better life.

As everyone began filing out, a strange muffled upbeat jangle was heard. Surprise registered in Bea's eyes. With clenched teeth, she whispered, "Aunt Jewels?"

"Yes, dear?"

"Please give me my cell phone."

"Certainly." Aunt Jewels began rummaging through her large purse. "I can't seem to find it, Bea."

Bea slipped her arm around her aunt's waist. "Because," she muttered into her ear, "it's wedged between the two caskets."

Aunt Jewel's drew back and her eyes grew large. "Mercy, you don't reckon....," and instantly broke free from Bea. Nervously she began shifting the pink roses from the coffin lid.

Immediately the Assistant Funeral Director was at her side. "Excuse me, ma'am, what are you doing?"

"I think my niece's cell phone is nearby."

"I don't think so!"

Once more the muffled sound rang out.

"There," said Aunt Jewels, "do you hear it?"

Gently his two gloved hands moved the coffin.

Plucking it up, Aunt Jewels shouted, "Here it is!"

Bea moved quickly, grabbed her cell phone, her aunt and hurried toward the front door.

"Please Bea, slow down. I'm sorry."

Bea's face was buried into her Aunts neck. "I have never, ever been so embarrassed in all my life. What were you thinking?"

Trying not to stumble, Aunt Jewels was taking tiny steps. "At the time I was saying to Roscoe I remember how lovely Laurie was. It must have dropped out of my hand."

"Where are you going Bea?" asked Jim.

"I'm not sure, but I want to get Aunt Jewels out of here."

While a bewildered look came across Jim's face, Aunt Jewels looked back over her shoulder, smiled and sweetly said, "Jim, please tell Roscoe I'll see him later. Bea is in a hurry!"

CHAPTER NINE

Aunt Jewels and Bea Go to the Library

As Bea turned off the ignition, she leaned back, sighed deeply and looked at her Aunt, seated in the passenger seat.

"What?"

"You realize we wouldn't have to spend time at the library, if it weren't for that dog."

"I'm sorry for Ramses chewing on your computer wires. I'm sorry for embarrassing you earlier."

"I know you are, but he could have been killed."

"Yes Bea…"

"Okay, come on. Let's do some research."

"What are you looking for?"

"I'm checking when Dinwiddle was in Angola and the write up's in the paper about retired Judge Joseph P. Wallace and his wife."

"Oh, Bea, there goes my cell phone. Hello? Yes, hello there. I'm with my niece at the library. When? Certainly. That could be arranged. I'd love to. See you soon."

"Who was that?"

"Roscoe. He's picking me up and we're going to have lunch at the Gulfport Yacht Club with his son Malcolm."

"I see."

"It's just lunch. Don't read anything into it."

"I'm not, only..."

"Only, what?"

"Has the FBI Agent been pushed to second place?"

"No, but he hasn't called either."

"Oh."

Aunt Jewels glanced toward the entrance door. "There's Roscoe. Give me a kiss, dear. Let me know tonight what you find out. Bye."

"Be careful." Bea gave a slight nod and wave to Roscoe as he waited outside the double glass doors.

Her aunt paused before going out, waved at Roscoe and then disappeared behind a nearby column. As Bea watched, she was puzzled by her aunt's actions. Once more she appeared, waved at Bea and then joined Roscoe on the other side.

Bea chuckled to herself and settled in, concentrating on her work. Hitting Google, she typed in '*Wallace murders*' and what seemed like ten thousand items popped up. She chose the first one. *On August 31, 1987...*

> *The coastal distinguished couple—he a federal judge, she a successful business woman and candidate for supervisor— were found dead in their immaculate mansion on Cedar Bayou Cove. Joseph P. Wallace had answered the door and had been shot from a silenced 38 Saturday Night Special. Lindsey, wearing a dressing robe, came downstairs to investigate. She was shot at close range. The murderer disappeared into the evening. Later on witnesses would tell police they had seen a dark navy BMW sedan in the vicinity several hours earlier.*

Bea clicked on the second article. It was a description of Lafouchfeye County after the 1969 Hurricane Camille.

> *Lafouchfeye County was one of the dazzling places along the Mississippi Gulf Coast. Gulfport was a quaint Southern town framed by century old houses and Spanish Moss-draped live oaks lining the beach. Lafouchfeye County however*

had a different life style. Drug-trafficking, prostitution, and gambling reigned in the back alleys and rooms along highway 90, known as 'The Strip'.

Because of a relaxed code of moral ethics among some officials, crime was unofficially protected and sanitized. The protests from its citizens went unnoticed. These businesses garnered revenue for the city taxes, so they were allowed to operate freely. Lindsey Wallace was looking forward to stopping all this activity. However, she didn't realize it was in her own backyard.

Bea clicked number three on the list. *Dinwiddle, Angola and Wallace Murders.*

When Lieutenant Lucas Ames, Gulfport Police returned from meeting with Dinwiddle at Angola, he and County Attorney Wendell Holmes Sr. reported their information to District Attorney Harlan Ladner, who suggested asking the U.S. Attorney to help in presenting the case. Dinwiddle informed them of another inmate named Semetski; better know as 'Smitty'. County Attorney Holmes Sr. made another trip to Angola with Captain Bob Larson of the Lafouchfeye County Sheriff's office who had recently been assigned to take over the Wallace murder investigation.

As she started to click number four, her cell phone vibrated. It was Jim. "Hello? I'm at the library. No, she went to have lunch with Uncle Roscoe and his son Malcolm. No, I can stop by. I love you too. Bye."

After paying for printouts, she headed for the double doors. The jangle from her cell phone caused her stop. "Hello? Yes, I'm fine. No, you just missed her. Oh, I see. You called, but she didn't answer. Mr. Thomas, my aunt had another engagement. Oh, you are in town. I'll see you there. I was going to the Sheriffs office myself. Bye."

CHAPTER TEN

Lunch with Roscoe, Malcolm and Aunt Jewels

While driving to the restaurant, Roscoe would glance over at Julia and grin ear to ear. "Julia, you look ravishing."

"Thank you," she gushed. "I must say I wasn't expecting a luncheon date so soon."

"My dear, I was going to mention it earlier, but I had another matter on my mind. Guess I developed a senior moment."

"Oh Roscoe, you? Never."

"I truly hope you don't mind the short notice. Malcolm will be surprised also."

"Why?"

"Because he's not expecting his dad to bring a lady."

"I'm looking forward to meeting him."

Roscoe gripped the steering wheel. "Julia, he has been a good son."

Affectionately patting his sleeve, she said, "I'm glad for you. Bea has made me proud too."

"Do you like Jim Travis?"

"Her fiancé, the Sheriff? Of course. He's a wonderful person."

"Have you heard anything about that couple?"

"They've identified them. Taylor Lipton and his wife. Clyde, his father was devastated."

"I can only imagine. Has the Sheriff gotten any leads?"

Aunt Jewel's eyes lit up. "Well, he made a plaster cast of a footprint. Dr. Tate..."

"Nathan Tate?"

"Yes, do you know him?"

"He has a solid reputation."

"Jim says that Nathan believes it was a heavy man who jumped out of that boxcar."

Roscoe chuckled. "He does, does he? And you saw an elderly man."

"Are you making fun of me?"

"No Julia, but you have described half of Lafouchfeye County. Remember, the entire country has labeled Mississippi as being obese. Oh here we are. There's Malcolm sitting inside waving to us."

Julia could see the apple didn't fall too far from the tree. As the two of them made their way to the back booth, Malcolm stood up and extended his hand. "Dad said he was visiting an old friend, but I didn't know his friend was such a lovely lady."

"You're just as charming as your father. My name is Julia, but my friends call me Aunt Jewels. I saw you at the banquet in Jackson."

"You were there?"

"That's right, with my niece Bea Winslow. She's a private investigator, you know."

Looking into his eyes, Aunt Jewels could almost see the neurons firing back and forth inside his brain. "I bet my father calls you Julia."

She laughed. "That's correct," and saw a familiar face enter the restaurant. "Oh look Malcolm, coming up the aisle. That nice man who was at the banquet also. Huett, something or other."

Malcolm looked at his father and said, "Huett Raleigh Cuevas."

"That's his name," said Julia. "Maybe he can join us."

CHAPTER ELEVEN

Retired Federal Judge Randall Penton and Mrs. Penton Have Lunch at Mary Mahoney's

Since Randall arrived first, he chose a table near the back. It was tucked in a secluded corner with a lovely view of the Mahoney garden and bird bath. A soothing waif of violin music circulated through the cozy room. Noticing his wife approaching, he stood up. "Ah, my darling, there you are."

"Randall, dearest, I was delayed because Aunt Lucy insisted we have tea. You remember, don't you? After all these years, she still is upset over the disappearance of her priceless jewelry."

Randall reached across the small table and took his wife's hand and nodded. "Yes love. But she adores you dearly and after all, you are her only living relative."

Eloise placed her other hand on top of her husband's and stroked it. "And her money will help your political ambitions."

He smiled. "I know. Are you ready to order?"

"I'd like a glass of white Chablis. By the way, did you visit with Wendell?"

"I'm glad you asked, dear. Wendell sends his best wishes."

"How is he doing these days?"

"Wendell? Oh he's fine, just fine."

Eloise slowly smoothed her napkin across her lap. "Was Matilda around?"

"Matilda?"

"Ms. Pettigrew, Wendell's lover."

"My dear, I didn't see a woman."

Eloise sipped her wine slowly. "I think I'm ready to order."

With a crook of his finger, Randall summoned the waiter. "We've decided on our lunch. I'll have the Shrimp salad, with Italian dressing."

Eloise ran her manicured nail over the small laminated menu. "I'll have the same, only with Ranch dressing."

"What's on your agenda for this afternoon, dear?"

"Aunt Lucy would like for me to stay over. She wants me to accompany her to one of the Casinos for a performance of the Cirque de Soleil. You don't mind, do you?"

Again Randall reached across and held her hand. "I'll miss you, but I understand. I can only hope you show me that much attention when I'm ninety-five."

CHAPTER TWELVE

Dinwiddle's Quik Stop

After Sheriff Travis drove away, Clyde turned and started walking toward the back room.

Teaspoon asked, "Why did you lie?" Clyde stopped dead in his tracks. "Because..." "I wasn't at your house and you know it." "But, you didn't kill my son and his wife either."

"Clyde, I was drunk and the train was headin' out of town so I got in one of the boxcars. When it slowed down and stopped, I jumped off. But I think I know who killed Taylor and his wife."

Clyde retraced his steps and grabbed Teaspoon by his shoulders. "Man, you have to tell the Sheriff."

"I can't. He wouldn't believe me."

Outside of The Quik Stop, a lone figure was lurking.

"Why?" Clyde asked.

"I'm a convicted killer."

"You were acquitted. Teaspoon, who do you think it was?"

As he passed the stocked counter, a shot pierced the window pane and almost struck him between his shoulder blades.

"Teaspoon!" Clyde cried and ran toward him. He screamed again, "Are you okay?" From his pocket, Clyde grabbed his cell phone.

"Sheriffs Office. Deputy Paulie speaking."

"I think so," answered Teaspoon and pushed himself up from the floor and leaning against the bottom counter.

Clyde saw the nape of his neck. "My God, you've been hit! Paulie, where's the Sheriff?"

"Right here. Why?"

"Someone tried to kill Teaspoon. Just now."

"Jim, Clyde's on the phone. He said somebody just tried to kill Teaspoon Dinwiddle. Shot him just now."

"Clyde, did you see anything or anybody?" asked Sheriff Travis.

"No, nothing."

"I'm on my way. Lock all the doors."

CHAPTER THIRTEEN ‐‐‐‐‐‐‐‐

Ms Matilda Pettigrew

Matilda dressed conservatively in a beige suit with matching shoes. Her hair was pulled back in a French twist. She began searching around her bedroom for a large matching purse. The biggest she could find. *Ah,* she thought, *this is perfect.* She filled the large bag with envelopes, baggies and packages that she had prepared.

After driving to New Orleans, she parked in the parking garage a block away from the bank and strolled leisurely along the boulevard, window shopping as she passed.

Stepping inside the bank, she removed her sunglasses and sought out the receptionist for the safety deposit boxes. After signing in, the box was opened and placed in the small room. Immediately she began exchanging packages, baggies and envelopes for the securities, bonds and bundles of cash. Matilda started to close the metal lid, but stopped. She reopened the box and one plush drawstring bag. A frown crossed her brow. There was only the gold bracelet. *Oh well,* she thought again, *nonetheless this is a small compensation for all that I've been through.*

She watched the guard replace the metal box and handed her the key. Confidently she strolled from the bank, across Canal Street and headed toward the Security Center. Lucy Dupree watched her from across the street.

There Matilda transferred all the items except the gold bracelet into another safety deposit box and returned home to relax by her pool.

Sometimes there wasn't a choice, but usually she preferred a younger man. Flipping her cell phone closed, she continued to stroll leisurely beside her kidney-shaped swimming pool, tapping the small black magnetic box which held the key, in the palm of her hand. Slowly she lowered her terry cloth robe, revealing a well-proportioned figure that had definitely been pampered over her seventy plus years. She leaned over and placed the box under the skimmer cover. A perfect hiding place.

She tossed aside her phone and dove into the cool blue water. This was one of the perks she had acquired from one of her many admirers. She loved swimming and had been a champion of the sport back in her college days. As she did the backstroke, her flaming red hair floated effortlessly, framing her face which soaked up the bright sunlight.

She loved her independent job of an Interior Designer. As she completed a lap, her thoughts were on the distant lands of Egypt, China, Mediterranean tapestries and rugs. Two more laps and she could bask on the cool chaise lounge.

While pulling herself out of the water, she noticed the French doors were open to the house. She quickly grabbed her robe and started toward the entrance. Judge Penton appeared. "Randall darling, this is a surprise."

"I thought it might be."

"Darling," she cooed, while caressing his cheek, "I wasn't expecting you this early. It was my understanding you had a luncheon engagement."

"I did."

"I see. Well now, would you like some wine?"

"Matilda."

"Yes? What is it?"

"Are you seeing Wendell?"

She brushed by him and proceeded towards the slate covered bar. "Would you care for red or white wine?"

Randall turned and followed behind her. "Matilda, I asked if you were seeing Wendell."

"I heard you, Randall. But it's not polite to ask a lady who her suitors are."

"I think it is proper Matilda, because I have devoted my life to you."

After pouring a glass of white wine, she devilishly presented it to him. "Randall, my darling, you have no reason to be upset. I have been exclusively yours for fifteen years."

He gently lifted the glass from her graceful hands and took several quick sips and placed it on the bar. "Darling, I'm going to get a divorce. I want us to be together."

Matilda tried to hide the shock which overtook her body. "Randall, a divorce would not accomplish our plans. What has happened for you to make such a rash decision?"

Randall grabbed his glass of wine and drank the last of it. "Haven't you heard about the bodies they discovered?"

"Of course, but I don't see..."

"Matilda, they could piece everything together."

She snuggled against his chest. "Darling, my sweet darling. Trust me dearest, you of all people have nothing to be afraid of. Haven't I always looked after you?"

Looking into her beautiful violet eyes, Randall murmured, "You are so beautiful. I could never let you go," and swept her up in his arms, carrying her off into the spacious bedroom.

CHAPTER FOURTEEN

Huett Raleigh Cuevas

All eyes were on Huett Cuevas as he walked through the entrance of the restaurant.   His size alone made him stand out. At 6'5", 275 pounds, he was a physical Adonis. He had played football on scholarships at Ole Miss and Harvard.

"Judge Blackledge, Malcolm, what brings you down to the coast?"

Malcolm smiled. "I might ask you the same question."

Aunt Jewels giggled a bit.

"My name is Huett Raleigh Cuevas."

"Huett," said Malcolm, "this is Ms Julia McKenna. She's an old friend of my father's."

"Well now, I'm certainly glad to make your acquaintance."

Julia smiled. "The same here, Mr. Cuevas. Would you care to join us? We were just getting ready to order lunch."

Huett nodded. "Gentlemen?"

Clearing their throats, both Roscoe and Malcolm agreed and proceeded to be seated. Malcolm repeated his question. "Like I said before, what brings you down this way?"

"Ms Julia," said Huett, "Malcolm is such a darn good lawyer, but he can be dogmatic about some things. I delivered an affidavit and I'm picking one up from Judge Holmes."

"My, my," declared Julia, "I had forgotten how interesting you lawyers can be."

"Have you seen Wendell this morning?" Roscoe asked.

"No sir. I have an appointment with him later on this afternoon. Malcolm, did you drive down?"

"I brought the yacht."

Julia's eyes sparkled. "You have a yacht?"

"Yes and no. Actually, it's my father's yacht."

"Oh Roscoe," she gushed, "After lunch, could we go aboard?"

"Why certainly, my dear. Malcolm and I would be more than happy to show you around."

Julia couldn't help but think about FBI Agent Jack Thomas. "You know, Jack Thomas has a yacht also."

All three gentlemen were surprised.

"Do you know Agent Thomas?" asked Huett.

Julia took a sip of wine. "Why yes, I do."

Roscoe adjusted his glasses. "How long?"

Julia stifled a short giggle. "My, my, you gentlemen are getting inquisitive about my friends."

"You'll have to excuse my father and Huett," replied Malcolm, it's just that we have known Agent Thomas a long time."

"Well," said Julia, "the dear man helped Sheriff Travis and my niece with a case of identity theft. He seems like a sweet soul."

Roscoe patted Julia's hand. "I'm sure he is."

CHAPTER FIFTEEN

Bea, FBI Agent Jack Thomas Meet at Sheriff Travis' Office

As Bea pulled up her white SUV in front of the Sheriffs office, she noticed a camouflaged World War II Jeep parked a few spaces down. "Umph," she muttered. "Could that be Agent Thomas's vehicle? Guess I'll find out soon enough."

Jim Travis stepped outside his doorway and grinned. "Hi there."

Bea furrowed her brow. "Hello yourself. Is this something special?"

"No ma'am. Just happy to see you, that's all. I saw you drive up, so I came outside. Come on in, Jack Thomas is here. You remember him, don't you?"

"Oh yes. Just talked to him briefly about twenty minutes ago."

Jim's eyes widened and he wriggled his arm around Bea's waist. "Now Jack, you're not trying to cut in on my territory, are you?"

Agent Thomas let out a boisterous laugh. "No, I don't want any Sheriff after me. Besides, I prefer a mature lady. Actually I was asking Bea where her aunt was."

Bea gave Jim a quick peck on his lips. "Okay guys, that's enough chit-chat. Jim, I found something at the library concerning Dinwiddle's incarceration at Angola," and she began digging into her briefcase. "I put it near the front so I wouldn't lose it. Ah, here it is."

Agent Thomas stepped forward. "Mind if I look over your shoulder, Jim?"

"Huh? Oh, no, no, not at all. Here have a seat."

"I'm confused, Ms Winslow," said Agent Thomas.

"About what?"

"Which homicide are you trying to help solve?"

Bea looked at the both of them and smiled. "All of them."

"All of them?" questioned Agent Thomas.

"Yes sir, because I believe they are connected."

"Even though there's a twenty year gap?"

Again she smiled. "Twenty-two."

Sheriff Travis cleared his throat. "Jack, the reason Bea believes the murders are connected is because of the similar M.O.'s and my father's notes."

"What notes?"

"His manila folder containing pertinent information on the murders of Judge Wallace and his wife, Lindsay," added Bea.

"The murders happened during my father, Cecil Travis' tenure as Sheriff."

"I thought all facts concerning that case were turned over to the FBI."

Jim answered, "Yes, they were, however my dad continued to investigate. No one ever contacted me, Jack, for more information and I've been Sheriff since January, 1988."

"May I look at them?"

"Sure, I'll get'em for you."

Bea propped her head against the palm of her left hand. "You're going to find the papers quite interesting."

CHAPTER SIXTEEN

Dinwiddle's Quik Stop

"Here Teaspoon, hold this white hankie against your neck," Clyde ordered. "I heard the Sheriffs Jeep drive up."

"What?"

"You heard me."

"How is he, Clyde?"

"It's just a flesh wound. A few inches to the right and he'd be dead."

Sheriff Travis bent down and took a long look at Teaspoon's injury. "Well sir, it looks like you have an enemy."

"Who would want to kill me?"

Clyde rocked backwards on his cowboy boots. "Well, it's darn tootin' somebody has it in for ya."

"Quit jackin' your jaws, Clyde, and help me over to the bench."

"If you two don't mind," said Sheriff Travis, "I'm gonna give a look around the porch."

As soon as the door closed, Teaspoon shot Clyde a look.

What?

"Clyde, you shouldn't have lied."

"But the Sheriff thinks you were with me and that's what's important.

Look, I don't want to know your business, Teaspoon. I don't care where you were."

"You shouldn't have lied, Clyde."

Clyde stuck both hands in his back pockets and rocked back on his cowboy boots again. "Okay Teaspoon, where were you?"

"Okay. By the way," said the Sheriff, pointing towards the side window. "I found this cartridge right outside, laying on the porch. If you two remember anything else, be sure to call."

"We'll do just that."

CHAPTER SEVENTEEN

Ms Molly McGuire

"You called for me Judge Holmes?"

"I did. What were you saying to our guests as they were leaving?"

Nervously Molly twisted the corner of her starched cotton apron. "I was just tellin' the young lady to say hello to her aunt. We are in the same garden club."

"You're sure that's all?"

"Yes sir. Oh…"

"What?"

"She did ask about the framed poetry in the foyer."

"What about it?"

"I told her it was a gift from Ms Pettigrew."

"Good. Now Molly, I'm expecting Mr. Huett Cuevas to be arriving shortly. If I happen to be indisposed, I would like you to receive the envelope he will be carrying. The package he will be picking up is lying on the credenza in the library. Do you understand all of those instructions?"

"Yes sir."

"The train has gotten off the track, so to speak, but with a little ingenuity, we can right the wrongs."

"Yes sir."

"You've been with me a long time, haven't you?"

"Yes sir, twenty-one years."

"I can remember meeting you for the first time, Molly. It was at Angola."

"Yes sir."

"He was a good man, your husband."

Molly felt her back bristle at his words. "He was a man of his word."

"Yes he was, my dear lady. That's why you have a job. I told him his family would always be taken care of."

"Yes sir."

"Maybe I shouldn't be asking you such personal questions, but Molly, do you ever go out for the evening?"

Again Molly began twisting her apron. "Out, sir?"

"Yes, dear lady. With a man, you know, a gentleman?"

"Not lately, no sir."

"So you do occasionally take in a movie with a man?"

"Not lately, no sir."

"I see. Stuart said he saw you strolling around the fountain in the park with a gentleman the other evening."

Molly smiled. "That was my cousin Toby, from my mother's side. He drove over from Moriah County and gave us some vegetables."

"That's right. You did mention the beef stew had fresh produce in it."

"Yes sir."

"Do we have any left?"

"The stew?"

"Yes."

"I believe so, sir."

"Good. If Mr. Cuevas arrives in time for lunch, we'll have the stew and some slices of the fresh baked bread you cooked."

"Yes sir."

"I'm glad we had this little chat, Molly. I like to keep in touch with my servants."

"Thank you, sir."

As she passed the foyer, she noticed Stuart standing off to the side. *He's been spying on her,* she thought. *Why else would the Judge be asking her all those questions? Could he know she's been seeing Teaspoon?   She would have to be careful.*

CHAPTER EIGHTEEN

FBI Agent Jack Thomas

After Sheriff Travis made copies of his father's file concerning the double homicide in August of 1987, Jack gathered up the information, jumped into his vintage Jeep and headed towards Diamondhead and home. He was shocked to see a dark blue BMW awaiting him in his driveway.

"Where have you been?" They asked.

He smirked. "Seeing...friends."

"Since when is Sheriff Travis a friend?"

"Does my being here bother you?"

"Yes, because you're up to something."

"Well, it shouldn't. How was your luncheon date?"

"Never mind about Julia. You leave her out of this, you hear?"

"Now you wouldn't want her to find out her old friend has a few skeletons."

"I'm warning you..."

Jack stepped forward. "Don't threaten me...," and suddenly his cell phone jangled. "Julia, what a pleasant surprise! Why no, no problem at all. I just arrived from spending some time with your niece and Sheriff Travis. I would love to. I'll bring the wine. Yes, I look forward to dinner also. Bye." Jack closed his cell phone and tapping it with his index finger, replied smugly, "I'd go home now if I were you, and think about your options."

With clenched fists Roscoe whirled around, got back in his car and drove away.

Jack continued walking up to his front door, flipped open his cell phone and punched in a familiar number. After several rings a raspy voice answered. "Hello?"

"Hi."

"What's up?"

Jack glanced around his surroundings. "I've gotten some important information about the Judge's murder in '87. Also I'm having supper this evening with Julia McKenna and her niece. I'll check with you later."

"Do you think they're suspicious?"

"Who? Oh, no. By the way, Roscoe paid me a short visit."

"Be careful, Jack."

----------------------------- CHAPTER NINETEEN -----------------------------

Huett Cuevas Visits With Wendell Holmes

After having lunch with Roscoe, Malcolm and Mrs. McKenna, Huett drove around for awhile. Since Malcolm had departed the restaurant before him, Huett wanted to make sure he wasn't followed. Waiting for the light to turn green, he checked his watch. It was almost time for his meeting with Judge Holmes.

He really didn't care for Wendell Holmes but Huett and Holmes's son, Wendell Jr. had roomed together in law school and become good friends. Also Emma Penton Holmes was Huett's cousin. He had been best man at their wedding. For the past twenty years, Huett thought their murder had been solved with Percy Dinwiddle behind bars. He was surprised when he was asked to accompany Taylor and his father, Clyde over to Angola Prison in Louisiana. One of Huett's informants concerning The Katrina Project was serving time there, so the guards were familiar with his face.

When he heard about the boxcar murders on T.V. and then later discovered it was Taylor Lipton and his wife, he was devastated. He recalled at the time, Malcolm didn't seem that upset and he wondered why. But again, thinking about everything, Malcolm had been acting strangely.

48

Before realizing it, he was on the road headed towards the chateau of Wendell Holmes. Driving up the circular driveway, he noticed someone peeking through the curtains of an upstairs window. As he pulled into the designated parking spot, Stuart, the butler came through the garden gate. "Hello, Mr. Cuevas. Judge Holmes is having tea on the rear balcony and wishes you to join him there."

"Thank you, Stuart." Huett stuffed his hands in his trouser pockets and slowly shuffled across the cobblestones which lined the pathway. As he approached the marble balcony, Judge Holmes sat before him relaxing on an olive green leather chaise lounge, smoking his stub of a cigar.

"Good afternoon, Mr. Cuevas," he said, waving his hand across the delectable food-laden cart. "Care for some iced shrimp and crab salad? My housekeeper, Molly, makes a mean dish of it. Some people swear it's the best on the coast."

"No thank you sir. I just had a delightful lunch."

"I know," he chuckled. "With Malcolm, Roscoe and Mrs. Julia McKenna, I believe."

"That's correct."

"How about some dessert then? Molly has some freshly baked cherry cobbler. Mr. Cuevas, you looked surprised when I mentioned your lunch companions."

"Yes, I was."

"I had briefly talked to Roscoe earlier and he had mentioned he was coming to the coast to see an old friend. Also, Malcolm had e-mailed me saying he was visiting Mr. Lipton at The Quik Stop and having lunch with his father. Please, have a seat."

Huett pulled back the Windsor chair and sat down. "If you knew Malcolm and his father were coming down, why did you ask me?
"

"To bring the affidavit? Because, I think it's time we got better acquainted. We didn't get to spend any time together at the banquet."

Huett nervously shifted about in his chair. "As I recall you were quite involved in a conversation with Judge Blackledge and Judge Penton."

"Again," remarked Wendell, motioning with his hand, "you are absolutely correct. That is why I wanted to spend this time with you. Now before you leave, I have a package I want you to deliver to a friend of mine. His office is near yours."

"And his name is?"

"How careless of me. Judge Ruben Glasglow."

"Isn't Judge Glasglow involved in a Katrina insurance investigation?"

"Is he? I wasn't aware of it."

"Judge Holmes, since Malcolm and I have The Katrina Project..."

"And also the late Mr. Lipton."

"Yes sir, I don't believe I should be having any dealings with Judge Glasglow."

"Huett, it's just a package. There's not anything dishonest in delivering a birthday present to an old friend. Molly? Molly!"

"Yes sir."

"Please bring me the manila envelope from the library."

"Yes sir."

When Molly returned with the envelope, Wendell snatched it from her hands and proceeded to open it. He grabbed the store-wrapped small package from inside and displayed it on the round marble table. "There, you see? A simple gift. Do you still object?"

Huett stood up. "No sir, I'd be happy to give it to him."

"Thank you Mr. Cuevas. Now if you'll excuse me, I have to get ready for my tennis date. Stuart will see you out."

After Huett was in his car, he took the tiny package out of the envelope again and looked at it. It looked innocent enough, but...

CHAPTER TWENTY

Sheriff Travis and Bea Winslow
at the Library

"Okay Aunt Jewels, what's up?"

"Whatever are you talking about, Bea?"

"The good china. The crystal goblets for water and flutes for wine...,"

"Jack is coming over for supper this evening. He's bringing Chablis."

"Oh..., I see."

Aunt Jewels cleared her throat just a little. "I don't suppose..."

"I could disappear for a few hours?"

"Could you dear?"

Bea grabbed her aunt in big bear hug. "Of course. Let me call Jim and see if he would like to take in a movie."

"I certainly hope he likes my smothered steak, scalloped potatoes, salad and peach cobbler."

"You keep talking about food and I might change my mind. Now get yourself busy. You have a guest coming."

Aunt Jewels was all a dither as she scampered up the stairs to her bedroom.

"Jim? This is Bea. Yes, I was thinking about you also. Do you have important plans tonight? Oh. Well now, that could be interesting. I'll meet you at the library in about thirty minutes. FBI Agent Jack Thomas is having supper with Aunt Jewels this evening. That's right. I'll see you there. Bye."

Fifteen minutes later, two headlights shone behind the edge of the house.

"Come in, Mr. Thomas," Bea said, smiling. My aunt is putting on her finishing touches."

"Something smells mighty good."

"That's her smothered steak. She uses her secret seasoning. You are in for a very gourmet dinner."

"I'm looking forward to it. You are joining us, aren't you?"

Bea actually blushed. "No, Jack. This is a dinner for two."

"I hope I'm not pushing you out of your home."

Aunt Jewels almost rushed down the flight of stairs. "It's not you Jack. She volunteered to be absent."

"I see," he smiled. "You want me all to yourself."

Aunt Jewels stifled a giggle.

"Well, I'll be on my way. You two have a lovely dinner and give a toast for Jim and me."

As Bea pulled out of the driveway, Jack wrapped his arms around Aunt Jewels and slowly drew her to him. "Julia, you are one desirable woman." and kissed her lightly on the cheek and then her lips.

A moment later, she looked into his eyes. "Jack, the food is ready."

He held her tightly against his chest. "My dear lady, at the moment I could live on love," and kissed her passionately.

All she could respond was with a weak, "yes...yes...yes."

At The Lafouchfeye Library

The library was deserted except for a few students huddled together in a distant corner. Sheriff Travis was first to arrive, so he headed toward the coffee shop. As he was paying for his latte, Bea walked through the sliding glass doors. "Over here, Bea," he whispered. "Want anything to drink?"

"Whatever you're having."

"Could we have another latte, ma'am?"

Bea glanced around. "Jim, why did you want to come to the library?"

"You haven't gotten your computer fixed yet, have you?"

"No."

"Well, Deputy Paulie spilled orange juice on our key board..."

"At your office?"

"Yeah, so it's out of commission."

"So you wanted to look at something?"

"Yeah, I thought you could pull up some more info about that double homicide back in 1987. You know, that Judge and his wife."

The young lady behind the cafe counter handed Bea her coffee and Jim his change.

"Thank you, ma'am. Okay Jim," pointing toward the only computer on the back table, "let's use that one."

First she pulled up Google and typed in *Judge Wallace murders.* She hit search. "There you are, Jim," and pointed to the many references.

"Gee whiz, that's a lot of information."

Bea nodded in agreement. "You'd think the killer or killers would have been caught by now."

Jim winked. "They are clever, but I agree with you honey, I think the Wallace murder case and these recent homicides are connected. Let's check this one out."

"You mean the one marked, *'Companion Club'*?"

"Yeah."

Bea punched in the title and up popped the following information: *A lucrative scam was coming from the Louisiana State Penitentiary at Angola. Want ads were posted in U.S. and Canadian papers targeting lonely men and women. Looking for companionship. Some ads specifically asked just men for men. Because of a network connecting convicts, prison guards, 'go-betweens' and others who lived outside of the prison area, thousands of dollars were being scammed from unsuspecting men and women. People were laundering the money through various banks.*

Bea hit print. "This is a good lead."

"So you think the dead Judge was in on this?"

"Yes, I do. Maybe he got greedy and wanted more. We don't know yet. Let's hit the next one that says *'FBI Investigates* V

> *FBI Special Agent Jack Thomas was curious about Wallace and Penton's secretary. Her name was Molly McGuire. She had no official secretarial training. At the time she was just the receptionist.*

Jim looked at Bea with questioning eyes. "Bea, is this the same Jack Thomas we know?"

"I guess so, unless someone else has the same name."

Jim looked puzzled. "He didn't mention anything."

"He wouldn't. He's FBI." "What else can you pull up?"

Bea's eyes scanned the side of the contents page. "Let's see now. Here we go. *'Wallace and Penton's Law Office'*."

> *FBI Agent Jack Thomas was astonished at all the phone calls which were coming out of Wallace and Penton's law office. Many were collected from Tunica. In fact one came in the day after the Wallace's murder. This meant someone at the law office accepted it.*

> *Thomas wondered why a respectable firm accepted "attorney-client" talks with a convicted murderer serving a life sentence; one who had no appeals left. Penton told Thomas that Tunica was the telephone exchange for Angola and the Louisiana State prison. Semetski, better known as 'Smitty', was a client of the law firm.*

Bea stopped and looked at Jim. "Just a minute, let me get something out of my briefcase. Here it is. Jim, where is Captain Bob Larson now?" Jim grimaced. "He died, remember?" "No, I don't."

"Yeah, he was chasing some bank robbers in an air boat across the Louisiana bayou. They said he was standing at the front. The boat hit a log and flipped him over. He went under the boat and was chopped to pieces. Why?"

"Because, he was assigned to take over the Wallace investigation."
"Oh..."

"We have to go now. Aunt Jewels is with Jack Thomas and their rendezvous has to be broken up."

"Bea, do you really think he could be involved?" "Right now, I'm more concerned about Aunt Jewels!"

CHAPTER TWENTY-ONE

Matilda Entertains for the Last Time

The candles were lit and soft, sensual music floated from the perfumed breezeway. Matilda watched as the headlights faded through the Spanish moss laden branches. She gingerly tapped the luminous crystal watch which encircled her petite wrist. *He's right on time,* she thought.

Picking the chaise lounge, Matilda gently reclined, positioning herself for his entrance. As he appeared through the garden and pool gate, he stopped and gazed at her lovely relaxed body. He started towards her and stretched forth both of his arms. Upon reaching her, she leaned forward, and slipped free of her soft terrycloth robe, grasping both his hands.

Instantly they merged into one as he lifted her graciously from the chaise lounge and began twirling around and around. He passionately kissed her neck, face and lips, whispering softly, "I love you so very much, so very much."

Matilda swooned as she turned rapidly in a circle. Her head became foggy due to the wine and prescribed medication. "Darling, I'm getting dizzy," she cooed. While spinning her, he carefully slipped one hand into the white latex gloves he'd hidden in his jacket pocket and then the other. He continued laughing and twirling her toward the deep end of the pool.

As her lover plunged them both into the blue water, she struggled, but his firm grip held her under. Her strong fingernails dug into his covered hands, but seconds later they went limp. He held his breath while watching the tiny bubbles escape her lips. Soon, it was over.

Throwing her over his broad shoulder, he climbed up the pool ladder and proceeded through the house to her bathroom. There he undressed her and propped her inside the bathtub, which he began filling with water. Hurriedly he ran back to the patio, retrieved her glass and the wine bottle, and returned to the bathroom, placing both on the ledge by her shoulder.

Pulling a large black plastic bag from his other jacket pocket, he placed her wet negligee inside. Leaning over the tub, he gently kissed her forehead and whispered, "Sorry lover," spread out the large bath towel and began undressing. When he had dressed again in dry clothes, he rolled up his wet clothes in the towel and headed toward the kitchen.

He stuffed the large towel with his clothes into the trash bag and removed the small metal shield from the hot water heater. Secondly, he strategically placed a saturated rag adjacent to the existing flame. Thirdly, he turned on the hot water faucet and the fourth step was the coup de grace.

Suddenly his ears heard the crunch of oyster shells. Someone had driven up. Quietly he tip-toed to the edge of the patio door. He watched intently as the driver started to immerge. My God! It was Eloise! Wait. What was she doing? She slid back behind the wheel and backed out. Quickly he ran back to the kitchen and turned on all the gas jets on the stove.

Driving away, he hummed to himself and thought of how the sequence of events would play out. The hot water faucet would cause the water heater to ignite the flame. This would catch the gasoline saturated rag on fire and the built up gas fumes would cause the explosion. Then he remembered the black plastic bag in the trunk. He pulled into a nearby child's playground and proceeded to peel off his torn blood-stained latex gloves and bury all articles in the adjoining woods, wondering all the while why Eloise changed her mind.

As he was finishing up, the explosion rocked the ground. He smiled.

CHAPTER TWENTY-TWO

Sheriff Travis and Bea Arrive at Aunt Jewels' House

As Jim and Bea pulled up in their respective cars, Bea noticed Agent Thomas's vintage Jeep wasn't there. Glancing through the kitchen window, she saw her aunt puttering around the table, clutching her chenille robe and holding Ramses, her little dog.

"Looks like she's okay," said Jim. The words were no sooner out of his mouth when the three of them heard what sounded like a large explosion.

Aunt Jewels and Ramses came flying out the back door. "What on earth was that?"

"Some kind of explosion," said Bea. "Are you okay Aunt Jewels? Where's Jack?"

Aunt Jewels held her robe and the dog tightly. "I'm fine," she answered, coyly. "Jack? Oh, he left about thirty minutes ago."

"Why? Anything wrong?" Bea questioned.

"Wrong? Nothing's wrong. He got a call and said he had to leave."

"Bea, honey," Jim winked. "I'd better check on that explosion."

"Aunt Jewels? Get dressed," ordered Bea. "We're going with Jim."

"I'll be back in a flash!"

Jim stepped into the kitchen, looked around and grinned. "Bea, honey, I don't think they ate dinner."

She arched one eyebrow. "Jim, I do not want to go there."

Aunt Jewels came bouncing down the stairs, with Ramses at her heels. She looked at Jim and then the fully set table. Marching by the both of them, she said defiantly, "He wasn't hungry!"

CHAPTER TWENTY-THREE

Roscoe Blackledge and Aunt Jewels
Drive to New Orleans, Louisiana

"Bea! Bea! Get up! It's in the paper. Bea!"

"What on earth are you yelling about Aunt Jewels? If we had any neighbors, they would be having your head."

"Look, Maude Benson wrote up the article. I knew when I saw her out there; she would be hunting around for news."

Bea poured herself a cup of coffee. "Now why are you acting like that? Maude's been writing articles for the Lafouchfeye Ledger a few months now. You were happy about it."

"I saw the way she was looking at Jack."

"So that's it. You're jealous."

"I am not!"

"What would you call it then? I noticed he kept his distance."

Aunt Jewels folded her arms across her chest. "He had work to do."

"Oh, I see."

"Anyway, look at this, it's in the paper. Second page, right hand corner."

"Are you going to hand it to me or do I have to arm wrestle you for it?"

"I'm sorry, here it is."

"Thanks. I thought I heard the phone ring earlier."

"You did. It was Roscoe. He's stopping by to take me shopping in New Orleans."

Bea folded the paper. "Now that's nice, Aunt Jewels. I hope you have a good time."

Her aunt picked up Ramses and placed him on her lap. "He even said I could bring my dog, if I wanted to."

"What's wrong Aunt Jewels?"

"Oh Bea, I acted like an old fool last night."

Feeling a bit awkward, Bea again folded the paper in half. "Dear, you know what I think?"

"What?"

"I think Mr. Jack Thomas took advantage of the situation, but don't put yourself in that position again."

Aunt Jewels stroked Ramses and giggled.

"What are you thinking?"

"Bea, I was laughing at your choice of words."

Bea smiled, finally opening the paper and began reading the article.

Woman's Death... Ruled Murder

By Maude Benson

Lafouchfeye County-

The death of a 75-year-old Jackson, Mississippi, woman whose body was found in her burned Lafouchfeye County home has been ruled a murder following an autopsy. Firefighters discovered the body of Matilda Pettigrew in the master bathroom of the fire-ravaged home. Forensic Pathologist, Dr. Nathan Tate of New Orleans, Louisiana said an autopsy performed the next day showed Pettigrew suffered multiple traumas by drowning and brain hemorrhaging. Tate said Pettigrew was "most likely" dead before her home caught fire. Authorities say the fire began in the kitchen and spread into the back bedrooms. Officials have determined the fire was arson. At present there are no suspects in the murder case.

Just then the land phone rang. "I'll get it, Bea. Hello? Yes she is, Jim. Bea it's for you."

"Hello? Hi, honey. He said what? Oh, I see. Well, Aunt Jewels is riding over to New Orleans with Roscoe. Sure, I'll ask her. Aunt Jewels?"

"Yes?"

"Dr. Tate said he has something very important to give Jim. He has a Seminar to teach and Jim has some business to take care of in Moriah County so he can't go over. Dr. Tate can't fax it either. Could you pick it up from Dr. Tate and bring it back here?"

"Sure, I'd be happy to. I know Roscoe won't mind."

"Jim, tell Dr. Tate Aunt Jewels will be there around one o'clock. Did he say what it was? Okay. Ahhhh, I love a mystery. Are you coming by for coffee? See you soon. Love you. Bye."

Aunt Jewels slowly lifted the cup to her lips. "What do you think he found?"

Bea continued to read the rest of the article. "Ummm, don't know Aunt Jewels."

Chapter Twenty-Four

Cahill Pettigrew

Since Aunt Jewels was going over to New Orleans with Roscoe Blackledge, Bea decided she would go back to the library and do some more research. Grabbing a cup of coffee, she proceeded back to the same computer she was on before. After hitting Google, she typed in *Wallace* murders. Instantly a crop of different topics appeared. She chose *Semetski.*

> *Back in the thirties, everybody knew who Al Capone was. In the late 70's and 80's, it was Sal "Smitty" Semetski that ran the Mississippi Gulf Coast. He was a native of New Orleans and his ancestors dated back to era of Huey Long. His first introduction to Gulfport was at the age of 18, a Seabee stationed at The Naval Construction Battalion Center.*
>
> *His father, Gesapti Semetski served as a jurist in the Louisiana State Senate before his placement on the Louisiana Court of Criminal Appeals. His mother, Ruby, was distinguished in her own right as a lawyer. His parents divorced when he was three years old. She remarried to an*

oil baron, 'Tex' Tyson from Texas. One of the founders of Al-Tex Oil Company. Through his mother's re-marriage, Semetski inherited a U.S. Senator, Roberta Tyson, for an aunt.

Even though wealth and prominence surrounded him, Sal or Smitty, as he was called, searched out the darker side of the underworld.

Smitty spent a good deal of his youth with his father at Louisiana State Prison. Since his father handled the district, the majority of prison personnel saw him for their jobs. Because of this introduction, later Smitty seemed to adjust quite well to prison life.

After his active duty service, his father told him to seek out a man by the name of Pettigrew. He owned a string of nightclubs situated along The Strip in Biloxi. Smitty and Pettigrew became friends.

Having been in the military, he regularly cheated the sailors who trusted him for some 'female companionship'. Yes, Smitty was certainly at the top of the heap for action. Bea was about to hit another source of information, when her cell phone rang. "Hello? Oh, hi Jim. I'm at the library. What? Who did you say was standing in your office? I see. No, no. I'm coming right over."

Bea surprised even herself at how fast she arrived at the Sheriff's office. There was Jim's old Jeep sitting outside and an antiquated bicycle. As she entered, her nostrils picked up the aroma of a cigar. Standing to her left was an older rotund gentleman, around 50 to 60. His weathered face indicated he had spent most of his life in a hot climate. He placed his cigar in an ashtray, smiled a toothy grin and stepped forward. "The name is Cahill...Cahill Pettigrew. I read in a California newspaper that my mother passed."

"I'm Bea Winslow, a private investigator. Won't you have a seat, sir?"

"If you don't mind little lady, I'll stand. I've been sittin' on a bus for four days to get here. Bought that old bike off a youngster in Gulfport. He told me how to get to the Sheriffs office here in Lafouchfeye County."

"Please accept my condolences for your loss, Mr. Pettigrew."

"I was tellin' the Sheriff here, my ma was a good woman. She raised me proper. I was one of those kids who didn't have a pa. Of course, I didn't know it at the time, but he was married. My mom was a beautiful woman and she loved pretty things. His promises didn't hold water. She didn't deserve to die like she did. That's why I came. To give her a decent burial and to find out who did it."

"Did you ever find out who your father was?" asked Bea.

"Yeah."

CHAPTER TWENTY-FIVE

Judge Ruben Glasglow's Office
Jackson, Mississippi

Even though Huett Cuevas was a distinguished attorney, he felt out of his element the minute he walked into the Glasglow building. Judge Glasglow's office was on the tenth floor, suite 1001. Stepping inside the elevator, there were assorted ladies and gentlemen surrounding him.

As they approached the tenth floor, all but one person got off. Huett glanced around at the five people who were walking ahead of him. One of them turned into the reception room of Judge Glasglow's office. He was second in line.

The pretty receptionist smiled after asking his name.

"Huett Cuevas, attorney. Yes, I have an appointment. Thank you." After waiting thirty minutes, Judge Glasglow's door opened.

There stood a portly, but well dressed gentleman in a dark blue suit with matching handkerchief and tie. A large gold and diamond ring adorned his right pinky finger. Black rimmed glasses and snow white hair framed his chiseled face. "Mr. Cuevas, please come into my office."

Huett picked up his tan briefcase and followed his directions.

"Please, have a seat. How are things humming down on the coast?"

After clearing his throat, Huett remarked, "Things are slowly getting back to normal."

"That Hurricane Katrina was something. You don't mind if I have a friend of mine sit in with us, do you?"

"No, Judge, not at all."

"Mary Beth, please have Ralph come in. Thank you."

"Mr. Cuevas, with all the shenanigans and corrupt people around, a person of my caliber can't be too careful."

"I totally agree."

"Hello there Ralph. This is Huett Cuevas, an attorney from Vicksburg."

"Nice to meet you Mr. Cuevas."

Huett recalled it was the same man ahead of him on the elevator and the first one to walk into the reception room.

"Now, Huett, what can I do for you?" asked Judge Glasgow.

"I've been asked by Judge Wendell Homes to deliver this package to you."

"Wendell sent me a package?"

"Yes sir. He said it was a present. A birthday present."

"Really. I've already talked to Wendell. He told me he thinks very highly of you. You're a bright young man with a splendid future ahead of you. I recall seeing you at the recent banquet hobnobbing with Wendell, Roscoe and Randall. Now about the present. Where is it?"

"I have it here in my briefcase." Huett unclasped the flap, pulled out his personal agenda date book and the manila envelope. "This is the package," and handed it to the Judge.

Carefully the Judge squeezed the small fastener together, opened the flap, and pulled out the store wrapped box as Ralph watched. As the Judge untied the ribbon, he said, "my mother always told me not to be anxious about unwrapping my presents. She was a great one for recycling ribbon and colored paper."

Once the folding was finished, he undid the paper fasteners on the side of the medium box. "I know Wendell and his practical jokes." Carefully the Judge opened up the container and pushed aside several folded sheets of paper. He stared at the contents, but only shared it with Ralph. "Was there any note with this?" asked Judge Glasglow.

"No sir," replied Huett; however I did remind Judge Holmes I was one of three who were involved in The Katrina Project and you were the presiding Judge for the insurance litigation."

"That is correct, Mr. Cuevas. I read in the paper one of your friends, a fellow lawyer with The Katrina Project was killed in Lafouchfeye County."

"Yes, Taylor was a good man and an excellent lawyer," Huett replied.

"That just leaves you and Malcolm."

"Yes sir. Although Malcolm graduated Harvard a few years ahead of Wendell Jr. and myself, we have always had an excellent relationship. Of course that includes his father, retired Judge Roscoe Blackledge. There is no doubt in my mind, sir, that our Katrina Project will have a positive favorable ruling. Good things will come out in the ruling. I certainly trust your judgment and your friend Ralph's.

"I'm glad I met you Mr. Cuevas. Now, if you'll excuse me, Mary Beth has lit up my private phone. No doubt it's 'the Mrs.' Ralph will show you out."

Huett closed his briefcase and started for the door. "I hope you liked your birthday present."

After Judge Glasglow watched Huett leave the reception area, he summoned Ralph back in his office. "Did you get all of that conversation?"

"Yes sir," said Ralph.

"Good. Notify Jack and tell him. Damn! He left his appointment book."

"Yes sir."

"Ralph?"

"Yes sir?"

"Use my private elevator to leave."

"Yes sir."

"Mary Beth?"

"Yes, Judge Glasglow?"

"Try to catch Mr. Cuevas. He left his appointment book."

"Yes sir."

As she waited for the elevator, Huett came out of the nearby restroom.

"Mr. Cuevas, you left your personal agenda book."

"Thank you ma'am. I admit I was a bit nervous with your boss."

"The Judge? He's a pussycat, but he can have big claws. Have you had lunch yet?"

Huett shook his head.

"Well then, let me get my purse and we'll go get a sandwich."

CHAPTER TWENTY-SIX

Roscoe and Aunt Jewels Return from New Orleans

As Roscoe held the kitchen door open, Aunt Jewels sashayed through, both hands loaded down with packages. "Bea, what are you cooking? It smells yummy!"

"Hi Aunt Jewels, Roscoe. Looks like you bought out the whole town."

Aunt Jewels sniffed the tangy aroma again. "Come on...."

"It's not me."

"I'm the chef for this evening," said Sheriff Jim Travis.

Again Aunt Jewels inhaled the tantalizing odor. "It's BBQ."

Jim walked gingerly past Bea and Roscoe, and then placed both his hands on Aunt Jewel's shoulders. "BBQ ribs like you've never tasted before."

She closed her eyes and sighed. "Are they almost finished?"

"Uh-huh. Just a few more minutes."

Quickly Aunt Jewels opened her eyes. "Before I forget," and she struggled with her purchases, "I have this thick envelope which Dr. Tate instructed me to give to you. Here you are, safe and sound."

"Thanks," replied Jim and stuck it in his shirt pocket.

Aunt Jewels looked puzzled. "Aren't you going to open it? He said it was very important."

He smiled. "After we eat. Roscoe, I bet she walked your legs off in the French Quarter."

Roscoe winked and grabbed Aunt Jewel's waist. "It was worth it." As Jim pulled out the mouthwatering rack of savory ribs from the oven, he yelled, "Okay folks, everything else is on the table. It's time to put on the old feed bag."

Of course at first everyone was too busy filling their plates to indulge in conversation, but a few minutes later, Roscoe asked, "did you find out anything about the explosion?"

Bea quietly took a sip of tea. "The house was totally destroyed; however Dr. Tate obviously found something."

Aunt Jewels lowered her glasses and pointed towards Jim's shirt. "I bet that envelope holds some mighty important information."

Again Jim smiled and patted his pocket. "Obviously."

"Well," she asked, "aren't you going to open it?"

"Aunt Jewels," whispered Bea.

"Well his note on the outside says it's very important," she muttered under her breath.

Roscoe patted her hand and reached for another biscuit. "Say, was Jack Thomas there?"

"Where?" asked Aunt Jewels.

"The explosion."

"Yes, he was."

Roscoe began buttering his biscuit. "I wonder why the FBI was involved?"

"Well, Roscoe," said Bea, "actually he told me and Jim he was in the vicinity when he felt the explosion."

"Good grief!" moaned Aunt Jewels.

"What is it?" asked Bea.

"I forgot my other bags. They're in Roscoe's trunk. Dear, please fetch them for me."

"I'll help you, Roscoe," said Jim.

"There's not that many, really."

"No problem."

As the trunk lid popped open, Roscoe began gathering bags and boxes on the right side.

"I'll get these three things on the left," said Jim, as he lifted two large boxes and a cloth shopping bag stuffed with small packages.

"Thanks," replied Roscoe, and began pushing down the trunk lid.

Jim snickered a little. "You know, you could have loaded some of these things in a few of those black plastic bags I saw in there."

"Right," answered Roscoe. "I keep those handy for buying plants at Home Depot."

"Good idea!" said Jim.

CHAPTER TWENTY-SEVEN

Bea and Jim Visit Percy (Teaspoon) Dinwiddle at the Quik Stop

Jim glanced around as he pulled up his Jeep in front of the Quik Stop. "Clyde must be gone, Bea. I don't see his old black dented truck around."

As they opened up the wooden screened door, Teaspoon was coming out of the storeroom. "Howdy folks, what brings you out this way?"

Bea smiled. "Jim wanted to check on you and see how you were doing. I sort of tagged along, you might say."

"Well, I'm happy you did, Ms Bea. A pretty face always brings a twinkle to my eye."

"Where's Clyde?" asked Jim.

"Oh, he got a telephone call from one of Dr. Tate's assistants, Alex Dedeaux, you know, about some more paperwork on Taylor and his daughter-in-law.

"I see," said Jim.

"Yeah."

"How have you been doin', Teaspoon?"

"You mean about gettin' shot at?"

"That's right."

"Old Doc Miller said it will heal fine. The bullet just grazed my neck."

Again Bea smiled. "I'm glad everything is okay, Teaspoon."

"Well Ms Bea, of course business always slacks off after the holidays. The first of the year is always a bummer. But my little store will make it."

"Sure it will," she added.

Jim grabbed Bea's arm. "Teaspoon, say hello to Clyde when he returns. Bea and I have to get back to my office. I just got a beep from Deputy Paulie."

"I'll do that. See you later."

"Just a minute," said Bea. "Teaspoon, I was doing some research at the library about the Wallace murders and I pulled something interesting up."

Teaspoon rubbed the back of his neck. "Oh, yeah?"

"Uh-huh. Didn't you know a 'Smitty' Semanski while you were in Angola?"

Teaspoon grinned. "Sure, everyone knew Smitty."

"He was a pretty Big Shot, right?"

Teaspoon shrugged his shoulders. "Some would say so."

"In some of my printed papers from the internet, it said you informed them of Semanski."

"Who is 'them'?"

"For one, Wendell Holmes, who was County Attorney at the time. For another, Captain Bob Larson who was with the Lafouchfeye County Sheriffs Office. However, he died in a tragic air boat accident."

"So?"

Bea moved closer to him. "Teaspoon, if you know *anything* about *any* of these murders, it would be to your advantage to tell me and Jim. One attempt has been made on your life. Next time you may not be so lucky."

"Bea, honey, Deputy Paulie paged me again. We really have to go."

Just as they were pushing open the screen door, a taxicab approached, and then the driver quickly shoved the gears in reverse and pulled away.

"I wonder what that was all about?" asked Bea.

"I don't know, honey." Let's go back to my office and check with Deputy Paulie."

CHAPTER TWENTY-EIGHT

The Lafouchfeye All Saints Chapel Services for Ms Matilda Pettigrew

On the morning of the services for Ms Matilda Pettigrew, it was extremely cold and wet. A steady downpour had begun around midnight, and had continued in a light drizzle. Slowly all the participants walked somberly into the chapel and took a seat in the various pews.

Of course Cahill Pettigrew, her son, sat up front. To give him support and comfort, Bea, Aunt Jewels and Jim sat beside him. Bea gave her Aunt a stern look and tucked her cell phone inside her jacket pocket. Aunt Jewels rolled her eyes. Two pews back, on the left side sat Judge Wendell Holmes Sr., his butler, Stuart, and housekeeper, Molly McGuire. On the opposite side were Judge Randall Penton and his wife Eloise. She intermittently dabbed her eyes with a lace handkerchief. The late arrivals sat in the rear. They consisted of Judge Roscoe Blackledge and his son Malcolm, Huett Raleigh Cuevas, Teaspoon Dinwiddle, and FBI Special Agent Jack Thomas.

As Cahill walked toward the podium, Judge Ruben Glasglow and his secretary, Mary Beth Nightingale entered and eased into the last pew.

Cahill cleared his throat and swiped his nose with a large red bandana handkerchief. He stuffed it back in the rear pocket of his faded jeans and waved his hands over the mourners. "I want to thank all of you for coming out on this awful, miserable day to pay your last respects for my mother, Matilda. Basically she was a good woman; she just fell in love with the wrong man. He was married and she was pregnant, with me.

She had me in California and at one time was an actress in a string of 'B' class cowboy films. But, he called her and she hi-tailed it back to Jackson, Mississippi. She left me with some friends of hers. Don't misunderstand now, she loved me and she said as soon as the money started rollin' in, we would be together. My father helped set her up in the Interior Design business and then introduced her to some high falutin' friends of his. The years went by quickly and soon I was out of school. I started workin' in a tourist place, panning for gold. It was a livin'. Every once in awhile I received a postcard, tellin' me she was doin' okay.

I was twenty-five when I decided to see her. I had been doin' some actin' myself, so I hopped a bus and went to Jackson. I remember askin' the cabbie at the bus depot if he had heard of Matilda Pettigrew.

He shot me a wide grin and told me "everyone knows Ms Matilda. She's a might pretty woman. Good business head too. Has her own Interior Design Shop over on Hawthorne."

I asked him to take me there. He told me he'd be glad to. And off we went. I remember when he drove up, I saw her through the large window pane. She was with a male customer. She briefly looked around and put something down the front of her blouse. A few seconds later a closed sign was placed on the inside of the door.

The cabbie chuckled, "I guess she's busy at the moment, sonny."

"I just asked him to take me back to the bus station. Well, that's enough memories. I'm here to take her ashes back to California and scatter them into the Pacific Ocean. Again, I thank all of you for showin' up."

As the Assistant Funeral Director stepped forward and presented the brass urn to Mr. Pettigrew, several of the participants came up the aisle to pay their respects to him.

"Excuse me," Jim told Bea and Cahill, "I want to catch Jack."

"Sure," they said in unison.

As he turned to go down the far left aisle, he patted his shirt pocket. Where was the envelope that Aunt Jewels had given him with Nathan's reports? Whew! That's right, he had taken it out when he went back to check with Deputy Paulie. Well, he thought, *I have to look at that after this is over.*

"Your mother was a lovely woman," remarked Wendell Holmes. "She was the decorator for my home. I'm sure our Sheriff will bring the fugitive to justice who did this dastardly deed."

Cahill politely shook his extended hand.

Eloise Penton was next in line. "You poor man. All those years you were neglected. We tragically lost our daughter, Emma. Your mother and I were not the closest of friends, but I wouldn't wish a fiery death on my worst enemy."

"And you are?" asked Cahill.

"She's Eloise Penton, my wife, and I'm Judge Randall Penton. Because of your mother's line of business, many of my constituents used her talents."

"So you knew my mother?"

"She was a business acquaintance."

Aunt Jewels had scampered down the farthest aisle and had managed to come face to face with Jack Thomas as he headed towards the exit. "Hello, Jack."

"Julia. I am happy to see you, but these are not pleasant circumstances."

Roscoe was watching the two of them.

"I was wondering what your plans were, you know later on?"

"I'm afraid I have some rather important business to attend to."

Suddenly, she just blurted it out. "Am I going to see you again?"

Jack politely tucked her arm in his and led her through the door frame into a secluded foyer. "Julia dear, of course you are. I adore you, you know that."

Julia felt her knees buckle. She couldn't figure what effect this man had over her. She whispered, "I was hoping I wasn't just a 'fling'."

He gently kissed her cheek. "I'll call you later, dearest," and then proceeded out the door, turning briefly to blow her a kiss.

"How sweet," said Roscoe.

Julia turned around, her eyes flashing. "Were you eavesdropping?"

"No, I just happened to be behind the dapper Mr. Thomas. Julia, you're my old friend and I don't want to see you hurt. Please be careful. He's a dangerous man."

"You're just jealous, Roscoe Blackledge because I've never had any serious feelings for you," and hurriedly walked outside and toward Jim's Jeep.

CHAPTER TWENTY-NINE

FBI Special Agent Jack Thomas

Aunt Jewels watched as Jack Thomas drove off in his vintage Jeep. *I wonder where he's going*, she thought. All three of them, Bea, Jim, and Cahill Pettigrew came out of the Funeral Home.

"Aunt Jewels," said Bea, "have you been waiting long?"

"No, not really."

"Anything wrong?"

"No, no I'm fine."

Jim asked, "Did Jack Thomas leave? I was trying to catch up with him."

"Yes, he left just a few minutes ago."

"He didn't happen to mention where, did he?"

"No, Jim."

Again Bea asked, "Aunt Jewels, are you sure you're okay?"

"I'm fine dear. I think I'll take a nap when I get home." She let the raindrops moisten her fingers "The rain makes me sleep anyway."

"Okay, people," said Jim, let's pile in my Jeep and I'll drop everybody off."

"What's your pleasure, Mr. Pettigrew?"

"You can take me to the bus station, if you will."

"The bus station it is."

Since Aunt Jewels' house was close, they drove by there first. Secondly, they delivered Mr. Pettigrew to the Sunset Limited Bus Station, in Gulfport.

"I really appreciate all you folks have done for me."

"No problem," said Bea. "If you need anything else, don't hesitate to call us. You have both our land phone and cell numbers. By the way, I asked you the other day if you knew who your father was and you said yes."

"That's right."

"Do you mind telling us?"

He rubbed the brass urn gently and said, "Glasglow, Ruben Glasglow."

"Thank you Cahill."

"Thanks again and I'll see you later."

As Jim pulled away from the curb, Bea said, "Well, that's a surprise. I thought maybe it would be Holmes, Blackledge or Penton. But Glasglow, that throws another name in for the equation."

At Aunt Jewels' House

Ramses was happy to see his mistress and jumped up to greet her. "Hi there little man," she cooed in his ear. "I've missed you, too. Really you're the only 'man' I can count on."

When she heard the car door slam, she was surprised to see who was walking toward the back door. "Jack, this is a shock. Are you lost?"

He laughed a hearty laugh. "My dear, I got to thinking as I was driving away and saw you sitting on the bench outside the funeral home. Jack, you are a louse. You know you care a lot for this woman and yet you know she feels rejected."

Aunt Jewels turned around with Ramses, and sat down by the kitchen table. "I certainly didn't feel chipper, I can tell you that." Ramses jumped off her lap and ran to the couch.

Jack reached down, lifted her up, and held her close to his chest. "Can you feel my heart, Julia? It's beating for you and only you."

Aunt Jewels felt her senses twirling around and a weakness creeping into her entire body. "Jack, I couldn't help but think you didn't care."

"My dearest, I care a lot, that's why I'm here. I'm worried that you are in danger."

After several passionate kisses, Aunt Jewels managed to whisper in his ear, "in danger of what?"

Again he smothered and blotted out her senses slowly maneuvering their bodies to the bedroom just off of the kitchen.

"Oh Jack, we mustn't, I shouldn't..." but all she heard was the slow staccato raindrops hitting the tin roof on the outside shed.

CHAPTER THIRTY

Bea and Jim Read Dr. Nathan Tate's Notes and Autopsy

Enclosed you will find my investigative report, autopsy and other pertinent documentation:

Case# 2357

Date: 02/15/09   Time: 2000

On the above date and time I received a call from Sheriff Jim Travis, Lafouchfeye County, Mississippi reporting the death of Matilda Pettigrew.

I responded to the scene and found the decedent lying in the master bathroom in her tub. She had been immersed in water, however, it is my belief the explosion jarred the plug and the water had ran out. The residence is a ranch type home. There was little blood at the scene.

I spoke with Sheriff Travis at the scene and he told me he heard an explosion around 1900 hrs. and found the decedent in the bathtub. The Lafouchfeye and Moriah County fire trucks were on the scene and had the fire under control.

My assistant Allison Keel and I saw a large amount of trauma to the decedent's head and arms.

Terry I. Miles

Enclosed are the photos I took of the scene and the decedent. Back at my lab the remains were weighed and tagged.

Located under the skimmer cover of the victims pool was a small brass key within a magnetic box. I am also enclosing such in a small brown envelope.

ANATOMIC DIAGNOSES

1. **Head and Neck**
   Abrasions of the neck Hemorrhage of the skull
2. **Torso**
   Bruises and abrasions
3. **Extremities**
   Defense-type contusions, abrasions and lacerations Upper and lower extremities Fracture, left hand

   The body is naked. A yellow metal ring set with a clear stone is on the 4ᵗʰ finger of the left hand. A large colored stone ring is on the 3ʳᵈ finger of the right hand.

EXTERNAL EXAMINATION

The un-embalmed body is that of a well nourished, well developed, female which measures 66 inches, weighs 145 pounds, and appears consistent with the listed age of 75 years. Extensive injuries to the head, neck, torso and extremities have been described.

GASTROINTESTINAL TRACT

The mucosa of the esophagus, stomach, and duodenum is otherwise intact; the stomach contains a small amount of mucoid fluid. The small and large bowels are unremarkable. The great vessels exit and return to the heart in a normal distribution and are unobstructed.

HEPATOBILIARY SYSTEM

The liver weighs 1480 grams and is covered by a dlistenina, intact capsule.

ENDOCRINE SYSTEM

The pituitary, thyroid, and adrenal glands are normal in size, shape, and location.

The body of Matilda Pettigrew expired on Thursday evening from drowning and brain hemorrhaging. She expired in her swimming pool and was placed within her master bathtub. This is where brain hemorrhaging took place due to a hematoma to her skull. Her stomach contents revealed a red wine and a light sedative. Even though the body was severely burned, a determination of several tiny pieces of charred latex rubber material was deeply wedged under two of her long fingernails.

DNA testing proved the blood found under her nails was not hers. Also of note, the killer moved both the bottle of wine and the glass the deceased was drinking from at her pool side to the master bathroom. I found a folded piece of lavender colored paper with the handwritten inscription by the deceased of a poem or verse. This was located underneath a chaise lounge near her swimming pool.   It is enclosed at the end of my report.

They apparently wanted to set the stage and have the investigators believe she carried both the glass and the bottle with her. Both were found completely intact. The victim's fingerprints were on both objects.

A particularly common form of death caused by asphyxia is, of course drowning. Drowned persons will show froth emanating from the mouth and nose.

When someone drowns, the air passages, as well as the stomach are filled with water. However, due to the pressure of water in the lungs, the blood vessels tend not to burst and rarely do petechial appear.

The obvious and fundamental difficulty about the forensic investigation is that it destroys even the evidence of its own origin.

Because we look at the way fire is investigated forensically, it is worth asking why some people deliberately set out fire-raising.   The answer, inevitably is that there are all sorts of reasons, but one of the commonest is the desire to conceal another crime, such as when a murder is committed and the culprit wishes to destroy the evidence including the body itself, or alternatively to give the impression that the deceased died as a consequence of what the murderer hopes will be taken as an accidental fire.

Date 02/16/09 Time: 9:25 am

Retired Judge Matthew C. Pettigrew presented a release signature as the brother of the deceased. I released the findings to the Judge.

The Verse:

If it be autumn when I die, I'll watch the shadows creep. And as you lie there sleeping, my memories I will keep.

As Jim was reading Nathan's notes concerning his investigation, Bea was scrutinizing every word on his Coroner Report. "Jim!"

Startled, he jumped. "Bea!"

Bea thrust the report towards him as he did the same to her. They were almost in unison as they yelled at each other. "Pettigrew isn't her son! He's her brother and a retired Judge!"

Jim grabbed the paper she was reading. "Yes, look at this date. He was over in New Orleans two days before he came here."

"Well I'll be," said Bea. "That's why Nathan wanted you to look at his findings."

Jim sheepishly looked at her. "We have to get him back here."

FOR LAFOUCHFEYE COUNTY, MISSISSIPPI OFFICE OF THE FORENSIC PATHOLOGIST, DR. NATHAN TATE NEW ORLEANS, LOUISIANA REPORT

CLASSIFICATION: <u>Homicide</u>   CASE:

<u>2,357 </u>DECEDENT: Ms Matilda Pettigrew

DATE REPORTED: **02/15/09** TIME REPORTED: **2000**

DATE OF DEATH: 02/15/09 TIME OF DEATH: **1900**

AKA: **MATTIE** OTHER I.D **NONE**

DOB: 12/03/34 AGE: 75 SEX: F RACE: CAUC.

EST HGT: 66" EST WGT: 145 HAIR: RED EYES: BLUE

BLOOD TYPE: A

ADDRESS:

CITY, STATE, ZIP: LAFOUCHFEYE COUNTY, MISSISSIPPI 39503 PHONE: 228-836-5555

IDENTIFIED BY: Brother

Terry I. Miles

OTHER INVESTIGATING AGENCY: *Sheriff Travis,*
<u>*Lafouchfeye County, MS*</u>

NEXT OF KIN

<u>*Retired Judge Matthew C. Pettigrew*</u>
<u>BROTHER</u>

<u>NAME OF NEXT OF KIN</u>
<u>RELATIONSHIP</u>

ADDRESS:__1235 Pinnacle Cove, Long Beach, California

RESIDENCE PHONE:_669-8956_BUSINESS

PHONE:

NOK NOTIFIED BY:_Monday, 7 A.M.

DATE:

CHAPTER THIRTY-ONE

Molly McGuire

It was getting late. If he didn't show up in the next few minutes, Molly was going to walk at least three blocks before hailing a taxi. *What was that sound*, she thought? Late at night, the park took on an eerie look. Branches waved in the breeze and lampposts cast shadows across the grass wet with dew.   She had tried to see him earlier, but when the Sheriff and Ms Winslow came out of The Quik Stop, she told the taxi driver to skedaddle.

"Molly?"

"Teaspoon, I was about to give up on you."

"I had to wait until Clyde left for his house."

"How are you feelin'?"

"Oh my neck hurts a bit, but Doc Miller said it would."

"Did you hear about Ms Pettigrew?"

"Yeah, that was awful. Do they know who did it?"

"I don't think so. Listen, the other night Judge Holmes had several of his friends over. I overheard them talkin'. Your name was mentioned."

"My name? When was that, Molly?"

Molly started counting on her fingers. "It was two nights ago."

"The same night someone took a pot shot at me through the window."

"Teaspoon, you gotta be careful, you hear?"

"Well now, Molly, you're in the rumble seat yourself."

"I know. He's already asked me several questions."

"Like what?"

"Am I seein' anybody?"

"You didn't tell him, did you?"

"Of course not. But I know he has Stuart watchin' me."

"Just in case old Stuart is nearby, let him watch this. Teaspoon grabbed Molly's shoulders and swung her around. Gently he planted a kiss on her lips that made her body turn to jelly.

"My, Teaspoon, that was unexpected."

He whispered in her ear, "I just wanted to make it worth your while as well as his."

"I agree," said Molly, and kissed him back.

CHAPTER THIRTY-TWO

Mrs. Eloise Penton

Softly the housekeeper said, "Mrs. Penton?"

"What?"

"Ma'am, would you like another glass of wine?"

"Would you please? The high ceilings in this library of Randall's holds the dampness."

"Would you like for me to stoke the fire?"

"Yes, yes, please."

"Is there anything else, ma'am?"

Eloise gathered the shawl tightly around her shoulders and then took several quick swallows of Yellowtail. "No, no, this is fine."

"I'll be going out to the market in a little while, for tonight's supper."

Eloise nodded in agreement and snuggled into the overstuffed chair. Her mind was racing now. Going from one scenario to another. First she thought of Wendell. He hadn't called her in two days. Did he find out she had visited Matilda? Then she thought of her deceased daughter Emma. That's why she was so emotional at the services of Ms Pettigrew. It was Emma's birthday. She would have been thirty-two. Of course, her mind wandered around to Randall.

As her eyes gazed at the flickering flames, she thought of another evening. Randall had just been appointed to the bench and they had attended a gala reception in his honor. He was ecstatic that night. Not only was he now a judge, but Wendell Holmes Sr. had also made him his law partner.

She remembered Wendell brushing her cheek with a kiss and whispering in her ear, "I would like to see much more of you."

Eloise stepped aside and snugly placed her arm around Randall's waist.

"Darling, are you all right?"

"Yes, dearest. Just letting you know how very proud I am to be your wife."

"Wendell," spoke Randall. "I'm the luckiest man in this room! A new partner, my appointment and a lovely, charming soul mate!"

Holding up his champagne glass, Wendell grinned. "I'll drink to that."

"Randall," asked Eloise, "could we possibly leave a little early?"

"I don't see how, darling. After all it's my party. Why?"

"Emma wasn't feeling well and I would like to check on her. Besides, the nanny had told me she had to leave at eleven."

"Wendell," said Randall, "would you mind driving Eloise home? She wants to check on our ten year old daughter."

"It would be a pleasure and honor."

The fog had rolled into the county and covered the entire area with a light muslin cover.

"Wendell, are you sure you're going the right way."

"Yes, Eloise."

"How can you see?"

When they came to the next stop sign, Eloise saw the muted lights of Dinwiddle's Quik Stop. "Wendell, this isn't the way."

"To my house, it is."

Eloise jerked her head towards him and begged him to turn around. But it was no use. Before long, they were in the garage and Wendell was pushing Eloise up the back stairs.

She was trying to struggle free of his strong grip. Through the kitchen and up the stairs to his master bedroom they went. She was whimpering like a young girl, begging him not to pursue his desires, but it was no use.

He poured her a small glass of brandy and ordered her to drink it down and then he began the ritual of undressing her. Eloise stood there numb and watched the black velvet skirt fall to the floor and then ever so gently he turned her around and began unbuttoning the ivory silk blouse, all the while caressing and kissing the nape of her neck. "Eloise darling, I have wanted you for a long time. Randall doesn't deserve your love and obedience."

Suddenly Eloise turned, facing him. Her tear-stained face began smothering him with kisses as she embraced him. Passionately their bodies intertwined and fell onto the huge bed.

About an hour later, they were headed towards Eloisie's house. She dozed while sitting next to him like a fitted glove. "Darling?" said Wendell.

"Yes?"

"You're home."

She waited for him to get out and then she slid out the driver's door. "Would you care to come in?"

"No, I should get back. We don't want to arouse any suspicion."

As Eloise started to kiss his cheek, he moved. "No my dear, no more romance tonight. Go check on Emma."

As the maid opened the front door, she called out, "Mrs. Penton, is that you?"

"Yes Margaret, I'm home."

CHAPTER THIRTY-THREE

At Aunt Jewels' House

The rain had stopped. Aunt Jewels could hear Ramses, her faithful little dog, whining and scratching at the spare bedroom door. She glanced at the lighted digital clock blinking. Nervously she wrapped the covers around her naked body and swung her legs toward the braided rug on the wooden floor. "I'm coming sweetheart. Momma's on her way."

As she scooted her bare feet across the floor, she caught sight of herself in the oval mirror. "Oh my," she muttered, while clutching her toga like sheet and primping with her hair. "Julia, what is wrong with you? What has happened to your common sense? Why can't you control your emotions when you're around Jack Thomas? Has he put some sort of spell on you? Look at yourself. Wrapped up in a cover, after a few hours of, well, never mind. I hope Bea and Jim don't return anytime soon." Again, Ramses shrill bark penetrated her thoughts. "I'm coming."

Opening the door, Ramses rushed in and jumped on the bed, wagging his tail in delight. Julia reached down and scooped him up with one arm. "You should be the only man in my life, but your mistress is a bit confused."

Ramses gently licked her cheeks and neck, spreading generous kisses.

"You have to be a good boy while momma takes a quick shower and gets dressed." For a few moments longer, Aunt Jewels playfully cuddled her small charge and then placed him back on the floor.

Aunt Jewels didn't hear the Sheriffs Jeep drive up, nor did she realize anybody was in the house until Bea yanked the shower curtain aside.

"Oh! Bea!"

"Aunt Jewels, the kitchen door was unlocked. Anybody could have walked in!"

Still flustered by her niece's actions, Aunt Jewels grabbed the towel at the end of tub and quickly covered her wet body. "Please, I'll be out in a minute. And put on a kettle of water. There's a chill in the air and I'd like a nice hot cup of tea."

Knowing better than to enter a lady's boudoir, Jim meekly asked, "Bea, is she all right?"

Bea came flying past him. "Oh yes, she's all right, for now. I may strangle her myself, after I give her a 'nice hot cup of tea!"

Jim's eyes surveyed the kitchen area. "There's two wine glasses by the sink and a little bit of Chardonnay left. Looks like Aunt Jewels had company."

A moment later, Aunt Jewels came into view, carrying Ramses close to her chest. Her reflexes tensed when she noticed Jim holding the wine bottle.

"Okay, Aunt Jewels," said Bea. "What's been going on?"

"Why?"

"Who's been here? Roscoe?"

"Roscoe? I haven't seen the dear man."

"Did Captain Eric come over?"

"What is this? The third degree or the inquisition?"

"Aunt Jewels, I realize you feel your business is your own, but..."

"And it most certainly is! I don't question what you and Jim do."

"But, I don't leave the door unlocked, either!"

"She has a good point, Aunt Jewels," said Jim.

In unison, both ladies replied, "You stay out of this!"

"For your information, Bea, it was Jack Thomas who stopped by."

Bea sneered. "Just for a glass of wine?"

Aunt Jewels arched one eyebrow. "He brought the wine."

"How convenient."

"Bea, I like him. He's a nice gentleman."

"Some gentleman. Woos you with a bit of the grape, and then beds you."

The tea kettle began whistling, so Aunt Jewels moved towards the stove. "Bea, at least I'm not sneaking around and, after all, this is my house."

"Put Ramses down, Aunt Jewels," ordered Bea.

Slowly Aunt Jewels lowered Ramses to the kitchen floor and resumed making her tea.

Bea lovingly put her arms around her Aunt and hugged her. "I love you dearly and worry about you. You're so trusting; you don't see the danger until it's at your doorstep."

Aunt Jewels drew back and looked at her niece. "I think Jack truly cares for me, Bea, I really do. Women can tell about these things."

"Did he tell you he once was a Judge?"

"No, but we haven't discussed his different occupations."

"What does he talk about?"

Aunt Jewel's eyes lit up. "About vacations and where he would like to take me. Things like that."

"Have a seat, Aunt Jewels. Jim and I want to tell you something."

"About Jack?"

"No, about Cahill Pettigrew."

"Oh, that poor man who lost his mother."

"Well now, he wasn't exactly telling us the truth."

"That wasn't his mother that was killed and burned?"

"Nope," said Jim.

Aunt Jewels sipped her herbal tea slowly. "Who was it?"

Jim poured himself a bit of the remainder of the Chardonnay. "Cahill Pettigrew is a retired Judge and that was his sister."

The teacup was still at Aunt Jewels' lips. "Mercy!"

Bea placed her hand atop Aunt Jewels' fingers. "Dear, I'm going to have to go to California and convince Mr. Pettigrew to return with me. That means you're going to be by yourself..., here at the house."

"I'll be fine Bea."

"I'd feel better if Jack Thomas wasn't so handy. And another thing. Aunt Jewels, you mustn't tell anyone where I've gone. Do you understand?"

"Of course I do, dear. I won't breathe it to a living soul." Again Aunt Jewels lifted the dainty teacup to her lips and enjoyed the warm liquid flowing down her throat.

CHAPTER THIRTY-FOUR

Retired Judge Cahill Pettigrew's, House in Long Beach, California

After Cahill deplaned in California, he snickered while walking briskly toward the Sacramento Terminal. Because of a personal visit, he had driven from Long Beach to the capitol and scheduled his return flight there. He thought to himself as he strolled along. *It had been easier than he had planned. They were nothing but hayseeds. All these years spent in community theatre and a few minor acting roles had certainly given him the advantage. Why, he had them eating out of his hands.* He chuckled while retrieving his luggage. *That Private Investigator, what's her name? Wins low. Bea Winslow and her Aunt. Oozing with Southern hospitality.* He had fooled them all. Just then his cell phone buzzed.

"Hello?" Yes, I'll hold. Hi yourself. No, no, the flight was fine. Picking up my luggage now. You don't say. Don't concern yourself, friend. Everything here is fine. I'll call you when I get home. Bye.

As he was making his way toward the exit, approaching him was a petite young woman, about thirty-five. "Mr. Pettigrew?"

"Yes."

She glanced both ways and said, "I apologize for interrupting you, but you've just returned from Mississippi, correct?"

"Why do you ask?"

"I was a close friend of your sister's. I used to live in Jackson, Mississippi; however, I married a... businessman who resides here, in Sacramento. I read about Matilda's passing.

"I appreciate your condolences, Ms...,"

The name is Cherie, Mrs. Cherie Kipper, Mrs. Robert Kipper."

"Again, thank you, but I really must be getting home," Cahill replied and nodded.

A sly smile crossed her face. "I understand. I guess I'll call that nice Sheriff, what's his name? Travis, Sheriff Jim Travis. Maybe he'll be interested in what I have to say."

"Look, Mrs. Kipper, I don't handle threats well at all, even if your husband is a Federal Judge."

"Why, Mr. Pettigrew," she cooed, stepping forward. "This isn't a threat." Batting her large black eyelashes, she snapped, "This is a promise!"

Cahill's demeanor didn't waiver. "Perhaps we can talk later, at my place. I assume you know my address."

"Oh sure."

"Good. I'll see you about nine this evening. Feel free to bring the Judge.

"I'll bring the wine and a friend."

CHAPTER THIRTY-FIVE

Roscoe Blackledge Visits Aunt Jewels

"Aunt Jewels? Are you decent?"

"Why?"

"Roscoe Blackledge just drove up. Looks like he traded his coupe for a four door model."

Slowly Aunt Jewels meandered down the wooden staircase. "He didn't call, Bea. Usually he calls."

"Maybe something urgent came up and he had to make a trip down here," replied Bea.

"He's at the backdoor now. Roscoe! Come in. Would you like a cup of coffee?"

"That sounds like a wonderful idea."

"What brings you down this way?"

"You."

Aunt Jewels blushed. "Me?"

"Yes, my dear. I've been thinking a lot about you... and me. Are you free for this evening?"

"What did you have in mind?"

"A spaghetti dinner at Luigi's and a movie."

As Bea poured coffee, she remarked, "Sounds like a winner to me, Aunt Jewels."

"Can I make one minor adjustment?" asked Aunt Jewels.

"Why certainly."

"Okay, dinner at Luigi's and come back here and pop in our latest DVD."

"Julia, I like that even better." He quickly drank his coffee and pushed back his chair. "I promised Judge Penton I would pick up something in Jackson for his wife. It's their anniversary. I'll be back to pick you up around seven o'clock this evening, okay?"

"I'll be ready."

He reached over and kissed her lightly on the cheek. "See you later."

"Bye, Roscoe."

Bea intently watched as he backed out of the driveway.

"Bea, what are you thinking about?"

"First off, I'm concerned about leaving you while I go to California and retrieve Mr. Cahill Pettigrew and second, I don't trust Roscoe."

"Bea, surely you don't believe Roscoe has anything to do with all these deaths."

"I don't want to believe it, but there are too many loose ends. For instance, Jim told me when he helped Roscoe with the packages you and he had brought back from New Orleans; he saw some black plastic bags."

"Ummph! Who doesn't have plastic bags in their trunk? Bea, you're barking up the wrong tree."

"Listen, I want you to be careful. I know Roscoe is an old friend...."

"And, Jack Thomas is a new friend."

"That's another one that bears watching."

"Well dear, what's on your agenda today?"

""I have to make my plane reservations and check with Jim."

"Let me get my drawers on and we will hit the streets."

Bea smiled and thought to herself, *I'm going to see if Maude Benson will stay with Aunt Jewels while I'm gone.*

CHAPTER THIRTY-SIX

Bea and Aunt Jewels Travel to New Orleans, Louisiana

Bea's cell phone began playing *Rhapsody in Blue,* while she and Aunt Jewels rode down the highway towards Jim's office. Bea looked at the caller I.D. "Aunt Jewels would you mind answering that? It's Jim calling."

"Hello? Yes, she's driving. You don't say! When? Yes, yes, it makes you wonder. No, we're coming to see you. I'll tell her. Bye."

Bea glanced at her aunt. "What did he say?"

Aunt Jewels' eyes danced with glee. "It seems you won't have to go to California after all to persuade Mr. Cahill Pettigrew to come back with you. Jim said Nathan just called and he spotted Mr. Pettigrew twice. Once earlier this morning when he had coffee at the Cafe du Monde, in the French Quarter, and later while he was making a deposit at the Orleans Bank."

Twice, Bea thought. She could hardly wait to get to Jim's office, zipping into the parking space and practically jumping out of her car.

Watching her, Aunt Jewels remarked, "My, my, we are in a hurry!"

"Jim," yelled Bea, "when did Nathan call you?"

Jim was standing there, holding the receiver of his land line. "Just a few minutes ago, why?"

"Call him back, now."

"Okay."

"What's the matter?"

Jim stared at the phone. "I was listening to a message..."

"Please, Jim. This is important."

"Okay," and he hit 'save' and then hung up. Quickly he dialed Tale's number. "Could I speak to Dr. Nathan Tate, please? Sheriff Travis, here. Thank you. Hello, Nathan? Bea wants to talk to you."

Bea smiled and mouthed *thank you.* "Nathan, you just called Jim and said you saw Cahill Pettigrew? Where? Cafe du Monde and the Orleans Bank. Do you know why he's back in town? I see. Aunt Jewels and I are coming over. Yes, please.   I'll explain when I get there. Bye."

Aunt Jewels' eyes were as wide as saucers. "Why are we going to New Orleans? I thought you were flying to California?"

"I don't have to, Aunt Jewels. Mr. Pettigrew has come to us and I think I know why. Thanks Jim," said Bea, and kissed his cheek. "I'm sorry if I sounded bossy."

"No problem, honey."

"You still have that phone recording, right?"

"Oh yeah, sure."

"See you later."

Jim walked behind them to the doorway and waved. "Take care of yourself and Aunt Jewels."

Downtown in New Orleans, Louisiana

"It turned out to be a lovely day, didn't it Bea?"

"Yes Aunt Jewels, it did."

"Now dear, when we see Dr. Tate, let me do the talking and remember, keep what we find out to yourself."

"Goodness Bea, who would I tell? The Garden Club ladies?"

"No, I was thinking of Roscoe and Jack."

"Oh Bea! Speaking of Roscoe, are we going to be back in time for me to go to the show?"

"Certainly."

"There's Dr. Tate, standing against that Barber Pole."

"And a parking space is vacant next to the corner. Perfect!"

After Bea and Aunt Jewels walked across the street, Dr. Tate stepped forward and smiled. "Hello there, ladies. Bea you sounded anxious over the phone."

"I am, Nathan. I think Cahill Pettigrew is looking for his sister's safety deposit box. Are you sure it was him?"

"He was sporting a fake mustache, but I was close enough to tell it was him."

"And he didn't recognize you?"

"No, he was too busy sorting through some documents. You mentioned a deposit box. Why do you believe that? You think it's here, in New Orleans?"

"That's right," and she produced a slip of paper with the possible numbers on it, plus the five letters. "Here, look at this."

Nathan began examining it. "Is this from the Wallace murders, in '87? What do you think the five letters are?"

"That's right. It's been unnoticed all this time."

"I can't believe the FBI didn't notice it. You realize Bea; the five letters could be a personalized license plate."

Bea gave a sly grin. "Nathan, they didn't know about it, whatever it is."

"How come?"

"Because they never asked Jim's father for any evidence."

"That seems unreal, Bea."

"I know, but it's the truth. Jack Thomas was totally surprised when Jim and I told him."

"I can imagine," said Dr. Tate and then grinned. "You know he was also a Judge at one time."

"Yes. Jim and I found that out. I believe the last three letters have to do with Pettigrew, but I can't figure out the first two."

"Well Bea, since we're right downtown, we'll check with the Royal Street branch. And then we can work our way around town. Aunt Jewels, I take it you came along for the ride?"

Her eyes lit up. "I just love detective work!"

"If your hunch is right Bea, he's already checked the main branch. You might as well ride with me."

As the three of them turned the corner, Bea's eye caught the headline on the Times-Picayune lying on the ledge of the corner newsstand... In big, bold black letters it read:

Judge Robert Kipper and wife killed in crash, Long Beach, California.

Judge Robert Kipper and his lovely socialite wife, Cherie perished in a fiery automobile accident on highway 101 in Long Beach, CA. He was a partner with Judge Ruben Glasglow, of Jackson, MS for several years before moving to the California coast.

At one time he and retired Judge Matthew Cahill Pettigrew Were co-owners of The Pettigrew Petroleum Company with Branches in Dallas, Texas, New Orleans, Louisiana and Biloxi, Mississippi.

Funeral services are pending due to notification of next of kin.

"Nathan! Look at this!" Bea yelled.

"Who is that?"

"I don't recognize the victim by name, but he was associated with Cahill Pettigrew and in a partnership with him." After paying the young man for the paper, Bea pointed to the printed article. "Look here, where it reads: Pettigrew Petroleum Company. Nathan, those three letters on the scrap of paper could stand for that."

Aunt Jewels squeezed in between the two of them. "You think so, Bea?"

Bea smiled. "Yes I do."

Nathan motioned for the both of them to head for his SUV. "If you are right Bea, and it is a safety deposit box, Cahill didn't find it at the main bank. Let's ride over to the Royal Street branch."

As the three of them entered the bank, Bea sought out the pretty receptionist, sitting off to the left. "Excuse me ma'am, could I talk to the Manager in charge of safety deposit boxes?"

"Certainly. That would be Ms. Lucy Dinwiddle. Please have a seat."

A statuesque brunette in a tailored suit approached the trio from the opposite side. "Good afternoon. My name is Lucy Dupree. I'm in charge of the safety deposit boxes. How may I help you?"

"I'm Bea Winslow, a private investigator, this is Dr. Nathan Tate, a Forensic Pathologist from here, in New Orleans and this is my Aunt Ms Julia McKenna. Actually, we were waiting for Ms Lucy Dinwiddle."

"Our receptionist has forgotten I recently got married."

It was as if Aunt Jewels had antennae embedded in her head. "Are you any relation to the Dinwiddle's living in Mississippi?"

Mrs. Dupree smiled. "I don't believe so."

Aunt Jewels was going to continue, but Bea gave a slight cough and produced a copy of the scribbled numbers and letters. "We believe this is possibly a safety deposit box that is in your bank."

Mrs. Dupree looked at the note paper. "Yes, we had those numbers."

"What do you mean, 'had'?" asked Bea.

"Are you from Louisiana?"

"My Aunt and I live in Lafouchfeye County, Mississippi, Dr. Tate lives here."

"Well then, I'm sure you have heard about Hurricane Katrina."

Aunt Jewel's eyes lit up. "We sure have! We stayed in our house!" Aunt Jewels continued to stare at Mrs. Dupree's lapel.

Mrs. Dupree pulled out a green bound ledger from the bottom left drawer of her desk and began flipping the plastic covered pages. Soon she had located safety deposit box 578 HCPPC. "When the levees broke, it flooded everything except here in the French Quarter. Consequently after the storm, we were able to come back." She grinned tapping her bright red polished nail on the number and letters. "I remember this one in particular."

"And why is that?" asked Dr. Tate.

"Because the second signature on the card came in and removed the articles."

Surprised, Aunt Jewels said, "There wasn't any water in here at all?"

"No, not a drop."

"I bet the owner was happy," chuckled Aunt Jewels.

"Mrs. Dupree, do you know who has this box? Have they returned to this area?" Bea inquired.

"Yes, to your first question and no, I haven't seen them, but you are the second person asking about this box and its contents."

"Someone else has been by, but not the owner?"

"Yes, yesterday. But he wasn't a relative."

"He wasn't?" said Bea.

Mrs. Dupree politely shook her head.

"Ma'am, I'm investigating several homicides and I believe that box is crucial to my case."

"I suppose with a court order, Ms Winslow, we could reveal the owners and its contents, however this particular safety deposit box has been transferred."

"And you can't tell us where or who has it without a court order."

"No ma'am."

"Thank you Mrs. Dupree for you assistance."

Aunt Jewels politely lifted her index finger. "Excuse me, could I ask a question?"

Bea's brow furrowed.

"I've been looking at your lovely brooch, Mrs. Dupree. It's simply exquisite. A golden daffodil surrounded by a sunburst of diamonds."

"Actually ma'am, it's a replica."

"Really? Well it's absolutely breathtaking. It looks like the real thing."

CHAPTER THIRTY-SEVEN

Sheriff Jim Travis Goes To the Library

After listening and writing the message down which the strange woman's recorded voice repeated several times, Jim filed his notepad in his inside pocket and headed for the library. Bea had showed him how to access the Internet and the information concerning *The Wallace Murders.*

Carefully he unfolded the piece of paper on which she had written the directions. In no time at all, Jim was right where he wanted to be. *Let's see,* he thought to himself, *which should I open up?*

Number Four—*More Clues.*

It was 1991 and four years had passed since that fateful, tragic murder of Judge Wallace and his wife Lindsey. Ironically, there was an abundance of energy generated for the second murder which took place four months later concerning District Attorney Wendell Holmes Jr. and his wife Emma. After Percy Dinwiddle was found guilty and sentenced to Angola for thirty years, it seemed people settled into a routine apathetic pattern of acceptance.

Several years later interest was generated by a group of law students from Harvard and more people came forward, claiming knowledge of the Wallace murders, but each lead would be a dead end. Some of these leads were from imprisoned men, saying they knew who the killer was and would say so if their own sentences could be negotiated.

Also the original investigators knew they only had one more year before the five-year statute of limitations would conveniently present itself for the scam charges. If an indictment wasn't made, the scam of the companion club wouldn't be useful. Something had to happen soon.

But nothing did happen. So as they say, the Wallace murders were placed in a cold case file.

Jim printed out his information and filed it within his inside jacket pocket. At the same time, he took out his notepad and read over the woman's recorded message again. "Sheriff Travis, I know who killed Matilda Pettigrew and Judge Wallace and his wife."

CHAPTER THIRTY-EIGHT

The Chateau of Retired
Judge Wendell M. Holmes

Wendell was stretched out on his comfortable chaise lounge on the back veranda of his chateau, sipping his latte. "Stuart?"

"Yes sir," replied the butler, as he scurried toward the raised Tuscan marble patio.

"Stuart, has the paper come yet?"

"I believe so, sir. I'll retrieve it from the kitchen."

"Judge Holmes?" alerted Molly.

"What is it?"

"Judge Glasglow is calling. Would you like for me to transfer it to your cell phone?"

"What's he calling for?" thought Wendell. "Yes, Molly, please do. Good morning Ruben. No, I haven't. Stuart hasn't given it to me. What? When? How did you find out? What did he say? No, I haven't heard from him or anybody. I will. Yes, yes. I'll keep in touch."

"Here's your paper sir. Will there be anything else?"

"No, Stuart."

"Sir, Molly will be leaving in a moment to pick up the fresh vegetables from Maude Benson."

Agitated, Wendell unfolded the paper. "Fine! That's fine; now go on with your chores."

The phone in the library began ringing. "Hello, Holmes chateau. Yes, I'll transfer you."

Wendell was startled by the cell phone ringing. He glared at the familiar number. "Yes. Yes, I just was informed by Glasglow. Yes, I'm reading it in The Lafouchfeye Ledger now. What are you talking about? You're not the hot shot detective you thought you were for all these years!"

"Judge Holmes," spoke Stuart coldly, "Judge Penton's car just drove up. Should I show him back to the veranda?"

Wendell was pacing now. Back and forth around the semi circle he walked. "Yes, yes, show him back here, Stuart." Wendell was surprised when he looked up and saw it was Eloise Penton instead. "Eloise!"

CHAPTER THIRTY-NINE

Bea and Aunt Jewels' Return from New Orleans

"Bea?"

"What?"

"You have been quiet the whole trip back. What's on your mind?"

"To be truthful?"

"Of course."

"I've been thinking about your movie date with Roscoe tonight."

"What about it?"

"I would rather you wouldn't go."

"Why?"

"Because..."

"That's not a good reason."

Bea turned off of I-10 onto Canal Road. "Because he could be the murderer of Judge Wallace and his wife over twenty years ago and Matilda Pettigrew."

"I don't believe it!"

"I know you don't, because you consider him a long time friend."

"That's right! I'm surprised at you, Bea."

When Bea approached twenty-Eighth Street, she stopped. When the light changed, she turned left and continued toward Jim's office.

Looking around, Aunt Jewels remarked, "I take it we're seeing Jim before we go home."

"Yes." Bea's cell phone began to quiver and dance across the dashboard. "Aunt Jewels, would you get that please?"

"Hello? Bea is driving. What? Sure. Yes, I understand. See you soon."

"Who were you talking too?"

"Dr. Tate."

"Why did you say we'll see him soon?"

"Because he wants us to drive back over to his office."

"Aunt Jewels you're not making any sense. We just left Dr. Tate."

"Don't you think I know that?"

"Well then, why does he want us to turn around and go back?"

"Because someone has killed Cahill Pettigrew."

"Just now?"

"I guess so. Sgt. Dan Beeson of Airport Security called Dr. Tate to tell him they found a man shot to death at the New Orleans International Airport. Dr. Tate sent two of his assistants over to pick him up."

"Aunt Jewels, get Jim on the phone. We have to let him know."

As she was carefully poking the numbers, she mumbled, "I guess my movie date with Roscoe just got cancelled."

Bea slowly glanced at her aunt. "Maybe you should learn how to speed dial on that thing."

CHAPTER FORTY

At Retired Judge Wendell Holmes' House

"Eloise!"

"I had to come Wendell. Randall hasn't been home for two days. I don't know where he's gone."

"I haven't seen him."

"Something dreadful has happened. I just know it."

"Would you like coffee or...something stronger?"

"Let me have a glass of sherry."

"Stuart?"

"Yes sir."

"Would you bring Mrs. Penton a glass of sherry?"

"Certainly, sir."

With a wave of his hand, Wendell dismissed his butler. "Now think Eloise. Do you have any idea what Randall had on his calendar?"

"Here's your sherry, ma'am."

"Thank you."

After taking several sips, Eloise placed the small aperitif on the glass tray. "Wendell, I believe he received a call from a Judge Kipper."

"He's in Sacramento, California."

Her eyes widened. "Do you know him?"

"I've heard of him."

"Randall told me he used to be in partnership with Judge Ruben Glasglow, in Jackson."

"Yes, yes, go on...," urged Wendell.

"He told him he must fly out there as soon as possible."

Wendell sat there with his fingers in a steeple position under his chin. "Who is 'he'?"

Eloise took a short sip of sherry. "I assume Judge Glasglow."

"Oh..."

"At first he wasn't going to, but he changed his mind."

"And he hasn't returned from that trip?"

Eloise began sobbing softly. "No, no, he hasn't." As Eloise reached for her sherry, she saw the bold headlines printed on the front page of the Lafouchfeye Ledger. "Oh my God!   My God! Wendell it says Judge Kipper and his wife are dead!"

"Eloise! Get a hold of yourself!"

"What did Randall do? Oh my God!"

"Calm down, Eloise."

"Calm down? Wendell, did he kill them and then kill himself?"

"Eloise, you haven't heard from anybody in California. Molly!"

"Judge Holmes, Molly isn't here," said Stuart.

"Stuart, I want you to make Mrs. Penton comfortable in the guest bedroom. She'll be staying with us for a short while. Eloise, you go with Stuart. He'll show you to your room. I want you to take a light sedative and relax."

Throwing her arms around his neck, she cried, "Oh Wendell, what would I do without you."

"It's going to be fine."

CHAPTER FORTY-ONE

Jim Meets With Bea, Aunt Jewels and Dr. Tate in New Orleans

"I got here as soon as I could," said Jim. "When did you find him, Nathan?"

Dr. Tate walked over to the stainless steel gurney on which Matthew Cahill Pettigrew was lying. "The police called me at 4:17 p.m. Bea, Aunt Jewels and I had just finished talking with Mrs. Dupree at the Royal Street branch of the Orleans Bank. It seems Pettigrew was going back to the New Orleans International Airport and somebody ambushed him in the parking lot. He was shot twice. Both bullets penetrated his chest and exited. The police are looking for the bullets."

Aunt Jewels was sitting comfortably in one of the cream cushioned chairs, while Jim and Bea were scrutinizing the victim's remains. "Did they find anything on him?"

"Yes, Jim. The usual things. Keys, wallet, credit cards and a note which had '87W-578-HCPPC written on it."

"I thought Cahill was our man," said Bea.

Jim agreed. "Well, we're back to square one, again."

Aunt Jewels motioned for Jim to come over. "Jim, I really don't like to look at dead people."

"Do you want to add something?"

"Well Jim, when we were at the bank, this nice lady, Mrs. Dupree, told us the bank didn't flood, and to find out anything we need to get a court order."

"Really?"

"Yeah, really, and another thing, we were the second person to inquire about the box. So, if Mr. Pettigrew asked about it and was not given access to it, maybe it wasn't his sister who put whatever is in there."

"You may be right, Aunt Jewels," said Jim. "Bea, you remember that phone call I received, when you came rushing in wanting me to call Nathan?"

"Yes."

"Well, it was from a woman, telling me she knew who killed the Wallace's and Matilda Pettigrew. I had Deputy Paulie check the phone call log and it came from a Cherie Kipper in Sacramento, California. Jack Thomas dropped by and just happened to see the records lying on my desk and told me he knew her and the Judge."

"Is Jack okay?" Aunt Jewels asked excitedly.

"Jack is fine."

"Jim, look at this," and pulled out the newspaper she had purchased earlier telling of the Kipper's death.

"Wow!"

"So she called you and then they turn up dead."

As Dr. Tate resumed his autopsy, he chuckled. "I'd guess you two are getting really hot as to who murdered whom...when!"

"Must be," said Bea, "because the killer or killers have been pretty busy!"

CHAPTER FORTY-TWO

Retired Judge Roscoe Blackledge Discovers Some Startling News!

Roscoe was surprised when Julia called him from New Orleans and told him she couldn't keep their movie/dinner date. She also mentioned Cahill Pettigrew's death. Since he was on the Coast, Roscoe figured he'd stop in and see Wendell. As he pulled off the main highway traveling towards Wendell's chateau, he turned and drove through central park. He saw the silhouette of what looked like two people arguing, possibly a man and a woman. He wasn't sure.

Quickly he came to a complete stop and cut off his high beams. As the automatic passenger side window rolled down, their boisterous voices became louder. Still, he couldn't decipher the gender. The blade glistened in the light of a nearby park lamp. After the thrust and jab, a low moan was heard, and one person slumped slowly to the ground. He heard a muffled scream and then... nothing. For a second Roscoe was going to rush across the damp grass, then he decided against it. He watched the killer swipe the long narrow knife across the smooth ground.

Roscoe restarted his vehicle and resumed his trip to Wendell's. He would call Deputy Paulie from there. Within minutes he was pulling up into the circular drive and making his way to the front door.

Roscoe was surprised when Wendell opened the door. "Well, hello there. What happened to Stuart?"

Stepping back, Wendell motioned for his guest to come in. "I sent him to Pooh's liquor store for some brandy. We are completely out." Wendell looked at his watch and then stepped forward to look down the road. "Actually he should have returned by now. What brings you out this way?"

"I was supposed to have a dinner date with Julia tonight, however, she's in New Orleans. It seems our 'friend' Cahill Pettigrew is dead."

"Dead?"

"Deader than a door nail."

"Have you seen The Lafouchfeye Ledger?" Wendell asked.

"No, why?"

"Look at the front page."

"Well, I'll be. Kipper and his wife." Roscoe took a step back. "I thought..."

"I had nothing to do with it, but, Eloise Penton, who is asleep in the guest bedroom, believes Randall flew out to California for a meeting with Judge Kipper and killed him."

"She's here?"

"Of course."

"Do you think that's wise?"

"Roscoe, she can't go back home. Not now, anyway."

"Do you mind if I use your phone?"

"No, why?"

"I witnessed a murder in central park."

"A murder? Right down the road from me?"

"That's right. Hello? Deputy Paulie? Roscoe Blackledge here. I believe a dead body, maybe two, are lying in Central Park, by the swing sets and children's slides. No, no I really didn't get a look at who it was. There were two, possibly three that I noticed. No, I don't know that either. I'm here at Wendell Holmes chateau if you need me. Thank you. Bye."

"You didn't see anything?"

"No Wendell, I just saw the outlines."

Again Wendell went to the front door and peered out into the evening mist.

Roscoe leaned against the foyer credenza. "Why are you so concerned about your butler?"

CHAPTER FORTY-THREE

Malcolm Pays a Visit to Dinwiddle's Quik Stop

"We got company," Clyde yelled, from up front. "Teaspoon, you back there?"

"Yeah, yeah, what?"

"I said we have company. Looks like that Blackledge fella."

Teaspoon came into view, favoring his right leg. "Hi there Malcolm. We don't get many visitors after the first of the year."

"Well, I missed seeing Clyde the last time I was by, so I just wanted to convey my condolences about Taylor and Laurie."

"I appreciate that, I really do," said Clyde.

"Do you remember a Cahill Pettigrew?"

Clyde scratched his head and remarked, "Wasn't that the feller who came here to see his momma?"

Teaspoon smiled. "You're right. What about 'em, Malcolm?"

"He was murdered in New Orleans."

Teaspoon snickered. "Someone is always gettin' murdered in New Orleans."

"Well, dad, Bea Winslow and Sheriff Travis seem to think all of these killings stem from Judge Wallace's murder in '87. That's really why I stopped by, Clyde."

"And why is that?"

"I was hoping either one of you could remember any little tidbit that would shed some light."

Teaspoon picked up a whittling knife.

Malcolm watched as he struggled. "Looks like your blade needs sharpening."

"Yeah, I can't find my regular one."

"Clyde, did Taylor ever share with you any of his findings about Teaspoon's case?"

"Not that I recall."

"How about you, Teaspoon? Did he share anything with you? Anything, at all?"

Teaspoon looked up from his whittling. "Nope. Say there Malcolm, looks like you've been trampin' through the marsh."

Quickly he pulled out a checkered bandana from his jacket pocket and began wiping the ribbing of his shoes. "I had a flat by the park."

"You should've called," said Clyde. "Teaspoon would've come to help you out."

Malcolm finished swiping off the last bit of mud, wadding up the handkerchief and stuffing it back in his inside pocket. Just then, his cell phone buzzed. He excused himself and walked outside. "Yes... I see. No, I'll take care of that. I said... don't worry. I'll call you when I get home."

CHAPTER FORTY-FOUR

Deputy Paulie Calls the Sheriff About the Murder

After the round table discussion in Dr. Tate's office between the four of them, Dr. Tate accompanied the trio to the elevator.

"That's my phone," said Jim. "Hello? Yes, Deputy Paulie, the three of us are just starting back to the coast. What? When? Where is Roscoe now?"

Aunt Jewels stifled a moan. "Has something happened to Roscoe?"

Jim shook his head 'no'. "I'll be there as soon as I can. Bye."

"What's happened?" asked Bea.

Flipping his cell phone closed, Jim replied, "Roscoe was on his way to see Judge Holmes and he saw a murder take place in Central Park."

Aunt Jewels muttered, "Oh my!"

"When Roscoe arrived at Holmes' chateau, he called Deputy Paulie. They met Deputy Paulie at the crime scene and found two bodies. Molly McGuire and Stuart Larson."

Dr. Tate snickered. "I guess you'll need my services. I'll call one of my assistants and follow behind you in the meat wagon."

"Mercy," said Aunt Jewels, That nice housekeeper of the Judge, and his butler."

"Come on, Aunt Jewels, strap yourself in. We've got to keep up with Jim and Nathan."

"Bea?"

"Yes?"

"What do you think happened?"

"I don't know."

"Well, if Roscoe was going to see Wendell and Wendell was home, he couldn't have done it."

"I'll admit it, Aunt Jewels. This one has got me buffaloed. I would have pinned my retirement check on Cahill Pettigrew as the murderer."

"But he's dead, Bea."

"I know that. What have you got there?"

"Oh this? Just the old recognition program for the lawyers and judges banquet in Jackson. Say Bea, did you notice the lovely pin that bank manager had on?"

"What are you talking about now?"

"At the bank."

"What about it?"

"The pin, Bea. It was just a replica, she said, but it was beautiful. A yellow daffodil surrounded by a sunburst of diamonds. It looked real to

me."

"No, no. I guess I wasn't looking. What's that you're looking at?"

"The recognition program from Jackson. You know, with the judge's and lawyer's names. It was lying up here on the dashboard."

"Let me see it."

"Sure, here."

"Aunt Jewels," said Bea, and slapped the paper down on the console between them. "Look here, at this name. Did you see him there?"

"Why, no. I had no idea."

"Try to get Jim on my cell phone."

"It's not going through, the battery is low.'

"Keep trying."

CHAPTER FORTY-FIVE

Aunt Jewels and Bea Arrive Back Home

As they turned off of I-10 onto Canal Road, Bea suggested they stop and get a soda from Dinwiddle's Quik Stop. "Looks like the place is closed." Within minutes they were traveling down the blacktop toward Central Park. Pulling in, and rounding the first curve, Bea noticed Jim's Jeep, Nathan's Coroner car, Roscoe's BMW and Dinwiddle's old black pickup truck. She parked her car near the park entrances corner granite stone.

"Watch out for the muddy marsh," yelled Jim.

Bea's heels sank quickly. "Now you tell me. Watch your step, Aunt Jewels."

"Mercy me."

Making a slight detour around the children's merry-go-round, Bea finally arrived at the scene. "What have we got?"

"Two vies," said Nathan. "One female, I'd say about fifty years of age, and...."

"She was older," replied Teaspoon. "Close to seventy."

"Thank you. And you are?"

"The name is Dinwiddle, Percy Dinwiddle. I've known Molly a long time. And you're welcome."

"And why do you happen to be here?"

"Clyde and I had closed up the Quik Stop and we were driving home when we heard the Deputy's siren. Clyde wanted to find out what was goin' on."

"And you're Clyde?" asked Nathan.

"Yes sir. Clyde Lipton."

"Please accept my sympathy in the loss of your son and daughter-in-law."

"I appreciate that," answered Clyde.

"Mr. Lipton, stay behind this yellow plastic tape and please don't touch anything.   Sorry Bea. Let me continue. The other is a male, about forty to forty-five. Both died of knife wounds to the abdomen. Could have been a murder - suicide but first we always consider it two homicides."

"Let me have a piece of that white plastic sheet, Jim," said Bea.

"Here you go."

"Thanks," and proceeded to spread it next to Molly's body. "Did you find her face up?"

"Yes," both men said in unison.

"How about the man?"

"He was face down," replied Nathan.

Bea placed her tiny flashlight firmly between her teeth and quickly examined Molly's fingers and hands. Jim knelt down beside her. "Look here, Jim. There are slivers of black plastic embedded under several of her fingernails, like she was dragging or carrying something."

Following the yellow crime scene tape, to the other side of the children's swings, Nathan yelled, "Over here!"

Jim jumped right up, but Bea took a little longer. "What 'ya got?"

"I believe the victim possibly discovered some evidence connected with Matilda Pettigrew's murder," said Nathan. "There's gasoline soaked rags inside this black bag and a bloodied negligee and gloves."

"Then what?" Jim asked.

"Deputy Paulie found a cell phone. He'll check the phone calls on it," said Nathan. "It could be that she was meeting someone here and while she was waiting, discovered the buried black plastic bag."

Bea was thinking out loud. "So her boyfriend shows up. No, it doesn't add up. Maybe the killer lured them here." Then she thought of something else. *Roscoe had black plastic bags in the trunk of his car.*

After Dr. Tate and his assistant Alex Dedeaux, took pictures, specimen samples, casts of footprints, they loaded up the two cadavers and the black plastic bag that was partially buried at the edge of the playground and drove back to the Forensics Lab in New Orleans, Louisiana.

Percy and Clyde were the first to leave, and then Bea and Aunt Jewels drove home, as did Wendell and Roscoe. Jim and Deputy Paulie went back to the Sheriffs office.

CHAPTER FORTY-SIX

Back at Aunt Jewel's and Bea's House

"Would you like a cup of hot tea, Aunt Jewels?"

"That would be nice. Have you spoken to Jim about the 'recognition program'?"

"No, not yet. He has two murders on his mind."

"So you don't think it was murder and suicide."

"No, I don't."

"Why?"

"Because Molly was seeing Percy and not Stuart."

"Really? How do you know that?"

"It's in Jim's file on Taylor Lipton's memos and notes. Molly used to be a part time secretary for Wallace and Penton's Law Firm. I also found it on the computer under *Wallace Murders*. Judge Holmes put her husband in Angola. That's where she met Teaspoon. After her husband died, she continued to visit Teaspoon. Several times when Taylor Lipton visited him, Molly had been there earlier. He has copies of the visitation sheets."

Aunt Jewels slowly shook her head. "Well I'll be… why do you think she was killed?"

"Possibly because she knew too much. Drink your tea. We have a busy day ahead of us tomorrow."

"Where are we going?"

"We're going back to the bank and follow up on that safety deposit box."

Back at Dinwiddle's Quick Stop

After opening up the back door, Clyde and Teaspoon ambled into the small four room cottage they shared in the back of the store. "Teaspoon," said Clyde, I sure am sorry about Molly. I know you were sweet on her."

"That I was, that I was."

"Did she have any kinfolk around here?"

"Nope."

"What's goin' to happen to her?"

"I guess after that Doctor finishes collecting what he has to collect, they'll put her in the ground in New Orleans."

"I think we should have a service here, in Biloxi."

"I'll call him tomorrow."

Back at Wendell Holmes Chateau

Eloise met both of the men at the garage door. "Wendell, where have you been? I woke up and no one was here."

"It's all right Eloise, Roscoe and I went for a short drive."

"Good evening, Roscoe."

"Hello, Eloise."

"Wendell, you haven't heard from Randall, have you?"

"No, I haven't heard anything."

"I was awakened by the phone ringing in the library. When I got there, it stopped. But it started again. I picked it up and someone asked for Molly, but she wasn't here."

Roscoe paused. "Eloise, did .the caller say anything else?"

"No, he just asked for Molly."

"Was Stuart here?" said Wendell.

"I don't think so. Why?"

"Wendell, you told me Stuart was picking up some brandy at the store."

"He was, Roscoe, but I thought he might have come home before..."

"Wendell, what is going on?"

"Eloise, Molly and Stuart were found dead in Central Park a few hours ago."

"Oh, my God!"

"Now, I don't want you to worry about this. You will be just fine here at my chateau. Roscoe has to go back to Jackson. Tomorrow I'll contact some friends and we'll see what we can find out. Meanwhile, why don't you fix yourself a sandwich." As the two men watched Eloise walk away, Wendell motioned for Roscoe to follow him into the library. Pushing some buttons, he pulled up the missed call. He recognized the area code and the number. "That's interesting."

"What is?" asked Roscoe.

"This number. It's Glasglow's office."

The Sheriffs Office Lafouchfeye County

As Jim and Deputy Paulie passed through the entrance, he heard the fax machine gurgling away. Deputy Paulie laughed. "Jim, I bet Dr. Tate is faxing you some info right now."

"I hope so!"

CHAPTER FORTY-SEVEN

Judge Ruben Glasglow's Office

He was already running late. His court date was 9:30. Hurriedly, Ruben rushed through the back entrance of the building toward the service elevator. He checked his watch once more. It was nine-fifteen. As he stepped forward, he caught his receptionist looking at him. "There you are, sir. You have a visitor."

"Please schedule them an appointment time. I'm late for court."

Just then Judge Randall Penton stepped into view. "Ruben..., I need to see you now."

Although he was shocked, he stayed composed. Pushing back his sleeve, his watch read nine-twenty. "Step into my office." Quickly, he opened up the outer door and dropped his briefcase, and then proceeded to his office. His furrowed brow said it all. "What is it?"

Randall paced and wrung his hands. "Ruben, I was with Robert and Cherie when they were killed."

"What?"

"Yes. I went out to California, just like you asked. We were driving into town. I was in the back seat. Robert was going around the curve. All of a sudden there was an explosion. I was catapulted out of the broken window. I remembered rolling and abruptly stopping. When I came to, my body was wrapped around a highway signpost."

Again Ruben checked his watch. Nine-thirty. "Does anyone know you are here?"

"No."

"Good. Wait here, in my office. I have to go to court. Don't leave. We'll figure this out." As Ruben started toward the outer room, he paused and turned around. "Randall?"

"Yes?"

"Does Eloise know where you are?"

He hesitated. "No." That was a lie.

"Good. I'll see you later." He picked up his briefcase and headed for the elevator. After pushing level one, he pulled out his cell phone and dialed. "Hello? Yes. Randall is in my office. That's right. I'll meet you later to discuss it."

CHAPTER FORTY-EIGHT

A Surprise Visitor for Judge Randall Penton

As he swung Ruben's office door open, he looked at the guest seated on the cushioned love seat. "Well, hello."

Surprise registered on Randall's face. "He's not here."

With a wave of his hand, he replied, "Who? Ruben? Oh, I know that. He called and told me to drive over and pick you up."

"Who's minding the store?"

"Who do you think?"

Randall folded the newspaper he was reading. "Where are we going?"

"Ruben thought you might like to go home."

"Yes, Eloise would be happy to see me."

The friendly visitor gallantly gestured with a flourish of his arm while holding the door open. "This way."

No conversation was initiated in the elevator. As they made their way through the parking garage, the happy visitor managed to click the lock open for the front seat. As Randall started to sit, he was blackjacked and shoved inside. "Sorry, old man," whispered his assailant. Instantly he grabbed the ropes that laid beneath the passenger's seat and began strapping Randall in.

A few moments later he walked briskly around the vehicle. As he slid into the driver's seat, he looked at Randall. "Look buddy, I'm afraid you're not seeing your lovely wife today."

CHAPTER FORTY-NINE

Bea and Aunt Jewels at the Orleans Royal Street Branch Bank

"Time to rise and shine Aunt Jewels."

"Already? I feel like I just went to bed."

"First we'll have some coffee and then we'll hit the Library."

"Bea, can't you go to the Library first and then come back and pick me up?"

"Okay, I'll give you a break." While making a single cup of Java, the land phone rang. "Hello?"

"Good, you're up," said Jim.

"What do you want at eight in the morning?"

"I was hoping you'd stop by the office. I got some interesting facts from Nathan last night."

"Well, I was about to head over to the Library and check on something. Care to join me?"

"Sure, meet you there. Bye."

Sitting in his Jeep, feet propped up and reading the paper. He was right on time.

Bea gave him a sly smirk. "For someone who has several murders to solve, you look quite content."

Jim grinned and reached out both arms for Bea's embrace. "No honey, it's not the murders, it's you and these hugs make me content."

She enjoyed being engaged to this tall, rugged man. "Well, let's roll over to the library."

~~~~~~

Jim plopped his large frame down on the tiny walnut chair. "What are you searching for?"

"Remember that newspaper clipping about the missing jewelry?"
"Yeah…"

"Well, I want to see if there's anything else written about it." Bea hit Google and typed *Estate Missing Jewelry in 1987* in the box. About twenty items appeared in the screen. "Let's try this one," and she clicked on it. No, that wasn't it, so she chose another. Again it proved the wrong one. "Well, like they say, the third times a charm," and she clicked away. "Eureka! Success!"

> *Speculation surrounding the missing brooch and bracelet belonging to Mary Necaise Dedeaux, sister of Lucy Shuttlesworth Cuevas and niece of Eloise Dinwiddle Penton has reached a plateau of great concern. It is believed to be apart of the criminal scam that led to the recent murders of Judge Wallace and his lovely wife Lindsey. Furthermore, a duplicate copy of the jewelry was made after their murders. Suspecting suspicion of a double-cross, the Judge and his wife were killed. Millions of dollars were involved and being laundered thru various businesses and enterprises and this is the reason the case remains unsolved today.*

"Well now, that's interesting."

Jim sipped his coffee. "How so?"

"How so? Eloise Penton was a Dinwiddle. The Manager of the safety deposit boxes was also a Dinwiddle before marriage to a Dupree. Aunt Jewels told me about a brooch on the manager's lapel."

"And you think it's all tied together?"

"I do."

"But honey, Teaspoon Dinwiddle was released because it was proven he didn't kill the Holmes couple."

"I know that, but it could be a cover up."

"So, you believe that's why Taylor Lipton was killed."

"I do. He was getting too close to discovering some important evidence. It has to be in that safety deposit box."

"So, you said you and Aunt Jewels are traveling over to New Orleans again to talk to the manager at the Royal Street Branch bank."

"That's right. I think she knows more than she's saying."

"Okay then, I'll see you later on this evening. I have lots of paperwork to cover."

With a short hug and peck, Bea breezed out the glass door and into her car.

_____

"Yoohoo! Aunt Jewels! I'm home! Are you ready?" As she popped out of the bathroom, Bea noticed the clingy dress. 'My, my, don't we look chic."

"I wanted that manager to know I could also dress fashionably."

"You have succeeded."

As they pulled into the bank parking lot, Aunt Jewels noticed Nathan's white SUV. "Look Bea."

"Wonder why he's here?"

Once they entered the bank, Nathan spied the two of them immediately. "Why are you both here?"

Bea's eyes scanned around the entire premises, noticing the yellow plastic crime scene tape stretched around the manager's desk. "To see the safety deposit box manager, Mrs. Dupree."

"I'm afraid you're out of luck. She was strangled a few minutes ago while taking a smoking break behind the rear entrance."

"Oh my!" wailed Aunt Jewels. "That poor woman!"

"Come on Aunt Jewels!"

"Where are we going?"

"To Hebron and find out what's in that deposit box!"

"But we need a search warrant."

"I'm going to try to bluff my way through."

"Oh my."

Just then Bea's cell phone jangled. "Aunt Jewels get it for me."

"Hello? Oh, hi Jim. Yes, she's driving. What is it?   Sure, transfer her. Hello? Mrs. Penton? Yes dear, this is Julia McKenna. Yes, my niece is driving at the moment. What?"

"What is it?"

"She thinks her husband Randall has been kidnapped."

"Kidnapped?"

Aunt Jewels' head was nodding with excitement. "You called Judge Glasglow in Jackson because he called the Holmes' chateau. I see, okay. You talked to the Judge's secretary and she told you Randall had been there, but left with who? No! Yes, yes, I'll tell Bea everything. Have you told Sheriff Travis? Okay. Where are you now? I see. Yes, go to the Sheriffs office. Bye."

Bea was gripping the steering wheel. "Well?"

"Oh dear, that was Eloise Penton. She thinks someone has Randall and they're going to kill him. He called her from Ruben Glasglow's office and when Eloise called back, his secretary told her an old friend had driven to Jackson to drive him home and he hasn't arrived."

"Does Jim know all of this?"

"Yes, she told him."

"Call Jim."

"Okay. Hello? Jim, Bea wants to know what you are going to do. I see, okay. He says we got a break. Old McDermott, the railroad inspector thought he saw a strange vehicle toward the back of the railroad yard. He didn't find any car, but Jim sent Deputy Paulie to investigate. What? What? Hello? Jim? It went dead, Bea!"

CHAPTER FIFTY

Lafouchfeye Railroad Yard

Randall was slowly coming to when they pulled into the rear of the railroad yard. His head ached and when he tried to move, he realized several large ropes held him tightly to the seat. "What are we doing here?" he asked.

The driver smiled. "You're going on a trip."

"No, please don't do this."

"Sorry Randall, but there's no other way."

"We've been friends for years!"

"You're breakin' my heart."

"Are you telling me, Ruben...?"

"Yep. You know too much."

"But I killed Pettigrew and the Kippers."

"I know and don't think me and the fellas don't appreciate all you have done over the years, but you were supposed to blow up in that car also. You were an excellent law partner and never complained. Okay, you complained sometimes when you had to get your hands dirty, but when Ruben told you to take care of Pettigrew and Kipper, you went without hesitation."

His eyes pleading for mercy, he begged, "Then don't kill me. Eloise and I will go away."

"Sorry old man, no can do. When Ruben saw you, well, he almost had to go back home and change his drawers. Okay, here we are. I'll come around and get you out. But first I have to gag you."

He watched as the railroad inspector crossed the last set of tracks and headed toward the small wooden shed propped up on several pilings. Methodically he maneuvered his body around the car, quickly opened the passenger door and placed the rolled up handkerchief in Randall's mouth. Then he slipped the outer ropes over his head and pulled him outside the car. "Don't struggle or I'll kill you right here."

Fear registered in Randall's eyes.

The driver pulled and shoved him along the railroad cars until he finally approached a partially opened boxcar. He lifted Randall up a bit and told him to pull himself up and inside. It was a struggle, but Randall managed to tumble and roll across the wooden floor.

"Good..., now get up and move over behind those metal crates stacked in the corner."

What seemed like hours were only minutes. "I have to leave for a few hours, so I'll leave you to reminisce about your life and the good times."

CHAPTER FIFTY-ONE

Orleans Bank.
Hebron Inland Branch
West Jefferson

Before getting out of the car, he checked his looks in the rearview mirror and straightened his patriotic tie. Tapping his slender mahogany cane, he moved with precision through the automated doors and over to the safety deposit box manager. "Good afternoon."

"Hello there. So good to see you again, sir."

"Yes, it has been awhile."

"I know you Judges keep very busy."

"Well, I haven't had those duties for some time, but nevertheless, my job keeps my mind occupied."

"I bet it does. What can I do for you today?"

"I came to retrieve the contents of my safety deposit box."

"Certainly sir. Would you step this way please? Did you hear what happened to sweet Mrs. Dupree?"

"Yes, I did when I stopped in to say hello at the Royal Street Branch."

"I heard she was strangled."

"Yes. Tragic. Very, very tragic."

"Here we are."

"Remain calm," he muttered. As he opened the lid, he saw a brick and several rocks. The gun was gone along with the bonds and securities. Only a few thousand dollars were lying loose. No gold bracelet. His eyes narrowed and he breathed heavily through his nostrils. Matilda! She did this!

He thought, *what was it Mrs. Lucy Dupree had uttered while he strangled her? Besides begging for her life, she was babbling something about security.* As her body slumped toward the pavement, he spied the brooch pinned on her lapel. Suddenly a rumbling noise appeared in the alley. A garbage truck was coming. He tried to snatch the pin, but the clasp held firmly. Damn!

Quickly he raced down the opposite end of the alley back to his car and phoned Judge Glasglow, in Jackson. "Hello, Ruben? I need a court order. Can you fax me the papers? Great! He flipped open his computer and printer, hooking them up to the lighter outlet. Within minutes it was up and running. He produced an embosser and voila! He smugly thought, *very official looking.*

He ran into the Security Center and approached the information desk. The clerk directed him toward the manager of the safety deposit boxes. He politely and firmly slid the document across the desk and watched her scan the certification seal. "Ah," she said, "Matilda Pettigrew's box." As the clerk left the vault area, he carefully slid the metal lid up and over. There was the gun that killed the Wallace's. The securities, bonds and $445,000.00 in cash. No gold bracelet. The rest was in a bank account in the Cayman Islands. He picked up his attaché case and began stuffing documents, paper, and money inside. Confidently he marched outside and handed her the box, key and a false inventory form as a receipt for contents. "It's been a pleasure, ma'am."

She smiled. "Say hello to your other half."

"Oh I will. I certainly will."

CHAPTER FIFTY-TWO

Orleans Bank,
Hebron Inland Branch
West Jefferson

"Hello there," said Bea. "I'd like to speak to the Manager in charge of the safety deposit boxes."

"Right this way, ma'am. Ms Papania, these ladies would like to talk to you about safety deposit boxes."

"My name is Bea Winslow and I'm a Private Investigator and this is my Aunt, Mrs. Julia McKenna. I have a search warrant to check box 578 HCPPC."

Ms Papania just scanned over the official looking document and smiled. "That has recently become available for rental."

Bea pointed her index finger to a heavily inked name. "Is this the owner?"

"Why yes. Such a nice gentleman, but there was another party also."

"Really? Who? May I know the contents?"

"Let me get the receipt of closure."

Aunt Jewels asked excitedly, "Would you make a copy for us?"

"Be glad to. Here you are. Is there anything else?"

"Yes ma'am. May I see the box?"

Aunt Jewels whispered, "Bea, what are you doing?"

"Just checking...," and proceeded to produce a clean sterile swab from her purse. All eyes were watching Bea. "There is one more thing, Ms Papania. Could Bea use your phone?

Without looking up, Bea said "Thanks.   Hello? Jim, my cell phone received no signal. Who kidnapped Randall? Gotcha! Yes, yes, Aunt Jewels and I have one more stop to make and then we'll meet you. Thank you again, Ms Papania for all of your cooperation and assistance."

As they stepped outside of the bank, Aunt Jewels grabbed Bea's arm and demanded to know what just happened inside was all about?

Bea smiled, "Gun powder residue."

CHAPTER FIFTY-THREE

The Showdown

Sheriff Jim Travis had Auxiliary Deputy Necaise back at his jail with the alleged murderer while he and Deputies Paulie and Tatum, approached the appointed place to meet with Bea and Aunt Jewels. He noticed a vehicle was absent and that worried him, so he and his deputies waited about 500 yards up the road.

Twenty minutes later, when one of the occupants had driven up, Bea and Aunt Jewels joined Jim and the deputies and the five of them approached the establishment.

The little bell jangled announcing that customers had walked into The Quik Stop.

From behind strings of colored beads hanging as a partition, Teaspoon appeared. "I thought I heard something. What can I do for you folks?"

The Sheriff tipped his hat. "Hello Teaspoon."

"I thought Clyde would be here by now. He said he had to run an errand," said Teaspoon.

"He won't be coming in," replied Sheriff Travis.

Aunt Jewels bobbed her head like a Cupie Doll and added, "Not for a long, longtime."

Teaspoon looked bewildered. "What's happened to him?"

"That's why we're here," said Bea. "He's in jail."

"In jail?"

"Teaspoon, Clyde Lipton killed Judge Wallace and his wife Lindsey, twenty-two years ago and then killed Wendell Holmes, Jr. and his wife four months later," said Deputy Paulie. "Sheriff Travis has all the faxes, documents and evidence in his briefcase."

Teaspoon stood there, stunned. "Clyde? The next thing you're gonna tell me is that he murdered his own son and daughter-in-law."

Deputy Tatum nodded affirmatively.

"I don't believe it!"

"It's true," said Aunt Jewels.

"Back in 1980," began Jim, "when Clyde was a young lawyer, Judge Wallace pulled some strings and he was appointed a Circuit Court Judge. Of course in payment, Clyde had to deal with the unsavory clients of Wallace and Penton, some of whom were in Angola Prison in Louisiana. Because of his involvement, he was convicted, fined, disbarred and served six years in a Florida prison. He vowed he would even the score."

Bea continued. "Clyde knew you liked your booze, would go into town and get liquored up and then crawl into a boxcar to sleep it off. Wendell Holmes, Jr., and his wife had visited his father that evening and told him he had uncovered some interesting information concerning the Wallace murders. Because they had visited your Quik Stop, Clyde knew they were in town. He made arrangements to meet them and he killed them."

Teaspoon sat there in disbelief!

"May I?" Jim asked.

"Certainly," said Bea.

"To continue," Jim added, "Clyde knew that you also had been a lawyer and judge and had run afoul of the law. He set you up as the scapegoat for his own murders of the Holmes'."

"But," said Teaspoon, "his son, Taylor, freed me."

"That's correct," said Jim, "when he did, Taylor discovered the information about the safety deposit box and the damaging evidence that would convict his own father!"

"So," added Aunt Jewels, "he had to kill them. Clyde knew when you went into town that night of February 17th; you would get drunk and ride the train home. He found out which boxcar you were in and called his son and daughter-in-law to meet him in the railroad yard. You were passed out behind several crates stacked in the corner. He shot them, with a silencer and poured acid on their faces and hands to slow down identification. First he dragged his daughter-in-law over by the open door. As he was dragging his son, you were beginning to awaken. Clyde had to hurry. Just then he felt a lurch and he knew something was causing the train to stop. He overlooked his son's cufflinks in his shirt and Laurie's bible. After the train stopped and you woke up and discovered their bodies, you jumped out of the boxcar. You were the one that I saw, but of course I didn't know it at the time."

"Remember, Teaspoon," said Jim, "When I came to see you and asked for your shoes and where you were between 10 and 11 pm?"

"Yes."

"Remember, Clyde said you were with him watching T.V.?"

"Yes, but I wasn't."

"I know," said Jim. "Because Clyde wasn't home. I had stopped by his house."

"Sheriff, I thought he was lying to protect me," said Teaspoon.

"I know."

"Who took a shot at me? It couldn't have been Clyde, because he was here in the store."

"It was Stuart, Judge Holmes' butler," said Deputy Paulie. "Dr. Tate faxed the Sheriff the results of the fingerprints he processed from the shell casing Jim found outside of the window at The Quik Stop. Both Clyde's and Stuart's were identified."

Bea added, "Teaspoon, Clyde knew you were sweet on Molly and he was afraid Molly would tell you about Stuart, so Clyde 'borrowed' your good whittling knife and killed Molly and Stuart. When Malcolm Blackledge had that flat tire in Central Park, he thought he'd have to kill him too. The plaster cast that Jim had from the boxcar murder and the ones he took at Central Park made a perfect match of Clyde's shoe. Clyde also had been seeing Matilda Pettigrew and she had promised him part of the 'scam' money her brother, Cahill, Wendell Holmes, Ruben Glasglow, and Randall Penton were involved in. His DNA from the blood he left behind on the plastic gloves and underneath Matilda's fingernails, also helped convict him."

Jim pulled out some documents from his briefcase. "Here, Teaspoon, are sworn affidavits from witnesses in Sacramento and Long Beach, California concerning Judge Robert and Cherie Kipper and Matthew Cahill Pettigrew in the scam of laundered monies from the 1987 murders of Judge Wallace and his wife Lindsey. You see, Judge Wendell Holmes Sr. ordered Randall Penton to eliminate Judge Robert and Cherie Kipper and Judge Cahill Pettigrew. After he killed Pettigrew, he blew up the Kipper vehicle. Yes, it was supposed to be a suicide mission. But Randall changed his mind. He couldn't kill himself, so he came back to his friend, Ruben Glasglow. This was a big mistake. Ruben called Wendell and he notified Clyde to travel to Jackson and get Randall. He brought him back and was going to kill him in the railroad yard after he picked up the money, jewelry, stocks, securities, the revolver and the expensive gold bracelet from the safety deposit box. He even bribed your cousin Lucy, who worked for the bank to help him. Then he killed her also. He told me, all of this while sitting in the back of Deputy Paulie's squad car. He called it tying up 'loose ends'.."

Teaspoon asked, "So, where's Clyde at now?"

"Well," said Aunt Jewels, "he's cooling his heels in Jim's jail. Old McDermott, the railroad inspector called Jim and told him about a suspicious car in the yard and he told Deputy Paulie to investigate. He found Randall Penton tied up and gagged in one of the rear boxcars. Boy oh boy, he began spilling all the beans! Paulie called Jim and they waited for Clyde to return to the boxcar in the railroad yard from picking up the loot from the bank. However, he discovered a double cross. Matilda Pettigrew had taken the gun, bonds, securities and several bundles of cash out of the safety deposit box and re-deposited it at the Security Center. When he discovered this, he knew he would have to get a court order. He told Jim and Deputy Paulie he called Judge Glasglow for his help. He then went to the Security Center and withdrew all the bonds, securities, and cash. When he returned to murder Judge Penton, they arrested him. He's been singing like a canary ever since! I bet if we tested that box at the Security Center, it would have gun powder residue too."

"Well," said Teaspoon, "It looks like I'm going to have to find me another manager for the store."

Just then, Special FBI Agent Jack Thomas walked into The Quik Stop. "So this is where everybody is. When I stopped by your office, Jim, and you were gone, I was concerned. I called Bea's phone and Aunt Jewels' house. There was no answer. That's when I really got worried."

"So," said Jim, "how come you drove out to Dinwiddle's Quik Stop?"
"I figured I'd ask Clyde. He always seems to know where everybody is."

Bea looked at Jack. "You should have looked through Jim's jail more thoroughly. Clyde doesn't have the answers anymore, and would you mind putting your hands behind you?"

Aunt Jewels' eyes flashed! "Bea! What are you doing?"

After she read him his rights and cuffed him, she politely said, "Aunt Jewels, I regret to tell you that your friend Jack is also involved in the 'scam' up to his eyeballs and has been for years." Bea abruptly turned him around. "That was the second mistake you made."

Jack smirked. "And what was that?"

"I was a criminal investigator with the FBI for thirty years."

"Oh, my stars!" Aunt Jewels wailed.

Deputy Paulie laughed. "This is getting to be a popular place. Judge Roscoe Blackledge just drove up."

When he stepped into the store and saw Jack Thomas in handcuffs, he smiled. "Hello, Julia. You okay?"

"I'm fine," she said softly.

"Roscoe, did Wendell take Eloise to the jail to see Randall?" Jim asked.

"Yes, he did."

"Good. Of course, they also are going to jail for their part in this."

"Roscoe," said Teaspoon. "Would you consider moving to Lafouchfeye County and being my day manager for The Quik Stop? Malcolm could park his boat down at the marina in Gulfport and rent it out for fishing trips."

Roscoe gave Julia a wink. "Actually it's my boat, but you have a good idea."

Just then a strange car drove up. In walked a dapper man, complete with white spats and a monocle. "I'm looking for a Mr. Percy (Teaspoon) Dinwiddle."

Teaspoon stepped forward. "That's me."

"Mr. Dinwiddle, I represent Poetry Unlimited out of Syracuse,

New York. My name is Thaddeus Underwood. I'm happy to tell you, you are our grand prize winner of the $250,000.00 poetry contest, with your poem, *'As You Lie There...Sleeping.'* I can definitely see you are busy at the moment, so if you don't mind, I'll come back."

"Certainly," said Teaspoon. "And thank you, thank you. See you later here at The Quik Stop."

"Well, well," said Bea. "We have a celebrity in our fair county. That reminds me, Teaspoon. Clyde tried to implicate you in the crimes by planting a verse of your poem with the victims."

"When did you enter the contest?" asked Aunt Jewels.

"Actually," Teaspoon paused, "actually I wrote that poem while I was in Angola. I showed it to Taylor on the day I was released. It was Taylor who suggested I send it in. I ran across it the other day as I was cleaning out a drawer. It reminded me of Molly and I clipped out the contest information and just dropped it in the mail."

Jim slapped him on the back. "I'm proud of you, Teaspoon, and by the way, I received word from Dr. Tate that Smitty Semanski passed away."

Teaspoon hung his head. "I'm sorry to hear that. Smitty, despite all his faults, was a good man."

"When do you need that day manager?" asked Roscoe.

Jim turned towards Bea. "Speaking of Dr. Tate, I wonder if that key they found under the skimmer cover at Matilda Pettigrew's pool has anything to do with that safety deposit box."

Bea's eyes flashed! "What key?"

Jim paused and swallowed. Hard. "Ah...the one that Dr. Tate sent back with his autopsy. It's in my evidence room."

Bea shook her head in disbelief. "Are you telling me, Jim Travis..."

Aunt Jewels sighed and closed her eyes.

"Looks like we have more company," said Deputy Paulie.

Jim smiled and pointed toward the entrance. "Well, I'll be. It's the Captain."

Shocked, Aunt Jewel's eyes flew open. "Eric?" she gushed.

"I stopped by the jail and Auxiliary Deputy Necaise said I could find everybody out here at The Quik Stop," said Captain VonBoatner.

Bea grinned. "We've missed you," and nudged her Aunt.

A sly smirk crossed his face. "Well now, after all when you run a cruise ship, they expect you to be on board." He sashayed over towards Aunt Jewels. "Did anybody else miss me?"

Bea coughed.

"Ummph!" Aunt Jewels remarked, and placed both hands on her hips. "You could have called or sent an e-mail!"

"Sweetie, I would have, but the systems were locked up."

"Well?" said Teaspoon, "what about it Roscoe? Do you want the job?"

"Yes, I'll take it."

Bea put her arm around her Aunt's waist and whispered in her ear, "Psst... look at it this way, they each have a ship."

Aunt Jewel's batted her eyelashes and smiled.

Manufactured By: RR Donnelley
                     Momence, IL USA
                     August , 2010